all the lies

BREAKDOWN

Peggy Webb

A Novel

Chapter One

Only twenty days 'til Halloween. Julia knew. She'd counted. Every October for the last five years.

As if she needed any reminders, ghoulish carved pumpkins decorated doorsteps, faux bats hung from trees, and ghosts lurked in every dark corner of her neighborhood – the one she'd deliberately chosen when she moved here. Nothing bad could ever happen in a neighborhood on a street named Harmony. On a quiet street where kids tossed balls at twilight and mothers stood in doorways calling them to supper, where the blue-ribbon school was just a few blocks away and the police station was within easy walking distance.

For that matter, nearly everything Julia needed was within walking distance. Until now. Until Dana Perkins had pulled her out of a safe rut and asked her to dredge up investigative skills from a life she'd left behind. One of Dana's students at Shutter Lake School was missing, and she would not rest until the girl was found.

Less than an hour ago Dana had pressed her again about the girl as they stood in front of City Hall where Julia's instincts told her Chief of Police Griff McCabe was lying about closing in on a killer. Everybody in Shutter Lake was up in arms about the town's first murder. How could Julia refuse? Her adopted paradise was in an uproar and so was her friend. It wouldn't kill her to drag out her investigative reporting chops and try to find the girl, would it?

Julia shifted her bag to a more comfortable position on her shoulder as she strode toward her cottage, a modest craftsman where culinary herbs grew on the kitchen windowsill and light poured through the windows in every room. Lots of light. Julia couldn't stand the darkness. Nor the pumpkins. Those grotesque masks. She wanted to walk up and slap every one of them.

She glanced around as if someone might have read her thoughts. Satisfied that her secret was safe, she climbed the steps and fitted her key into the lock on her front door. It was painted bright yellow, the color of hope, and beyond was Julia's orderly cocoon.

The ornate Victorian wall-hung mirror in the hallway showed a tall, slender woman on the wrong side of forty with long blond hair windblown and blue eyes untroubled. Julia Ford, lifestyle columnist for the *Firefly,* a weekly newspaper few outside of Shutter Lake had ever heard of, a paper she'd have dismissed as insignificant before she came here.

She nodded at her reflection, satisfied. Her mask was still in place, but that didn't mean Dana hadn't seen right through her. She was the school principal, a *psychologist,* for Pete's sake. She could spot a lie a mile away, even if it was just a little white one. Why had Julie ever told Dana, of all people, she'd ask for help from her former friend in the FBI, *former* being the operative word?

For reasons too numerous to even think about, Julia would never ask Patrick Richards for help of any kind, professional or otherwise. She could find that girl all by herself, thank you very much.

She kicked off her shoes then padded barefoot across dark oak hardwood floors to her kitchen and the Eastlake sideboard she'd found at a hole-in-the wall store in nearby Grass Valley. Good Stuff, the owner called the store, an apt name for a converted warehouse filled with antiques that would cost twice as much in New Orleans or New York.

Julia filled a mug with hot water from her Keurig then made her favorite drink, green tea chai from a mix she ordered online. No offense to Nolan Ikard down at The Grind. Or to Dana, who was practically addicted to his Macchiato Espressos.

Fading light coming through the stained glass in Julia's kitchen window turned her walls a rainbow of soft pink and gold. She loved that about California - the mild weather and the perpetual sunlight that gave Shutter Lake a golden glow.

Until the glow got tainted by murder. And now a disappearance. A runaway? A kidnapping?

She carried her drink into the sunroom she used as an office – deep wicker chairs with daisy print cushions, glass-topped tables scattered about and littered with magazines on antiques and gardening and music, a small French country desk with a comfortable swivel chair tucked into the corner. Julia flung open the curtain, set her drink on the trivet she kept on her desk and powered up her computer.

"Let's see where you're hiding, Josie Rodriguez."

A photo in the society pages of an earlier issue of the *Firefly* showed an exotic dark-eyed teenager, now seventeen according to Dana. Her uncommon beauty was set off by a lace gown and pearls, compliments, no doubt, of the Windermeres who flanked her. The caption underneath read *Benefactors of Shutter Lake Symphony Orchestra with Exchange Student.*

Josie was named only once in the full page article about Katherine and Quentin Windermere, her host family who not only funded the city's symphony but also its community theater and ballet. The arts community had other benefactors, of course. The town was filled with wealthy families who had distinguished themselves in the fields of science and medicine, mathematics and technology. But none gave so generously as the Windermeres, nor made a point to attend every concert, ballet and play performed in Windermere Center for the Arts. The imposing Grecian-inspired structure had been built entirely with their money in the heart of downtown Shutter Lake.

Julia knew this first hand. She was a great lover of music, a passable singer and a better than average pianist. She never missed an arts event in Shutter Lake and had interviewed the Windermeres many times in the last few years.

She grabbed pen and pad and started writing. *Symphony, Katherine W.*

Her cell phone blared out "Crazy." Her mother's signature ring. Not surprising coming from a Tennessee-born woman who grew up in the town Patsy Cline helped make famous. When Julia was ten her mother packed them off to Chicago where Rachel proceeded to become the belle of the Windy City.

"Mom? What…"

"It's all over the news about that poor girl's murder. I think you ought to come home where you'll be safe."

Julia's mother never said *hello* when she called. She just barreled into whatever subject she had on her mind, completely abandoning the Southern manners she trotted out with regularity in public. Rachel Maddox Ford Chin was nothing if not the Grand Dame of Chicago society.

Julia pictured her mother, an older and shorter but more elegant version of herself, standing in her expensive penthouse apartment - a modern conglomeration of glass and steel - and gazing at a sweeping view of the Windy City's skyline. Her blond hair would be swept into a French twist and she'd probably be dressed in slacks and one of her ubiquitous silk blouses, tucked in to show off her still-trim waistline. She would *definitely* be biting off her pink lipstick while she twisted the ever-present rope of pearls around her neck.

"Mom, if I were any safer, I'd be dead. This is the first murder in Shutter Lake's history, and even if I wanted to write about crime, there's none to report."

Until now.

"I'm *glad* you're writing about Beethoven and beef stew instead of cat burglars and serial killers. And so is Joe. He thinks you ought to come home, too. I'd just die if anything happened to you out there in the wilds."

"I'm not in the wilds, and nothing's going to happen to me."

Even as Julia said it, a wave of homesickness washed over her. Eating hot dogs in Wrigley Field, made as only Chicago can. Browsing museums with her mom. Sailing on Lake Michigan with Joe and that bossy Lhasa Apso he named Sweetie Pie, which said everything you needed to know about the man who'd been the only real father Julia ever knew.

"That does not make me feel one bit better, Julia. That poor dead girl probably thought she was safe, too."

"Her name is Sylvia. Sylvia Cole."

Was. Past tense.

It hit Julia hard that the very thing she'd run from had finally caught up with her — crime, the more sensational the better for the media. She'd covered that beat for years for the *Chicago World,* the *Tribune's* and the *Sun-Times'* biggest rival. Too many years to think about. Too many memories.

Julia pushed them aside and took a long, fortifying drink of her green tea chai. It had gone cold, but that didn't matter. She wasn't as picky about her drinks as Dana.

"You see?" Her mother let out a sigh that bordered on drama-queen level. "That's just what I'm talking about. That pitiful departed soul was somebody's little girl, just like you're mine. My *only* little girl."

"According to all the black balloons I avoided like the plague on my last birthday, your little girl is over the hill, Mom." Her mother chuckled, as Julia had intended. "Is Joe there?"

"Not yet, but he'll be here in about fifteen minutes. Let me run and get some tea then we'll chat 'til he gets here."

Julia almost let out a dramatic sigh of her own. "I can't. I've got things to do."

"What can be more important than talking to your mother? Maybe Joe can talk some sense into you."

Julia would love to talk to him, if nothing else just to let the lilting sound of his voice conjure up happy memories of a childhood spent tagging along behind him, asking a million questions. He always answered with the patience of Buddha. Her stepfather would press his case for her return, but in a way that was soft-spoken and polite.

A way that reminded her of Chief of Police Griff McCabe. And the entire falling-down house of cards that had once been the nation's perfect city.

"I really have to go, Mom."

Before Rachel could marshal any more arguments, Julia said goodbye and ended the connection. Her computer had gone into rest mode and she brought it back to life.

"Let's see what else you've been up to, Josie."

School events and academic awards in math, science and music. She'd been a star student with an incredibly bright future, which made her disappearance all the more puzzling. The selection process for exchange students was rigorous at the prestigious Shutter Lake School. After winning one of the coveted spots why would a girl making such stellar grades give it up? Especially when school was in session?

Julia continued to scan the articles. Josie had been photographed in more public appearances with the Windemeres. She had the kind of face loved by a camera lens. And she made the philanthropic white-haired couple, a handsome pair, look even better. No wonder the press always aimed a camera at her.

"Pictures never tell the true story." Had the Windermere's been using their exchange students to make them look good? Was their well-documented philanthropy an attempt to hide a dark purpose?

She printed off a good headshot of Josie and made a note to call Katherine Windermere for an interview. Symphony season was in high gear, with a fundraiser planned on the park for Saturday.

She had the perfect angle to question the woman.

The Windermeres had been on Julia's radar for some time now, well before Sylvia's death. The parade of foreign exchange students going in and out of their home had put her instincts on high alert. With Josie's disappearance, she could no longer ignore her intuition. She knew how to segue from music to a missing teenager, and she had a knack for getting people to reveal more than they intended.

Julia continued her cyber search and her note taking in the methodical, from-the-ground-up manner that had served her well in her days of investigative journalism. With a jolt she realized she'd missed this. Periodically her former editor emailed or called to lure her back. He wanted her full-time again in Chicago. Lately, he'd said he would settle for freelance in Shutter Lake.

Big stories, though. Not her current life-style pablum. His words, not hers.

It wasn't until her stomach rumbled that she realized she'd missed supper, whatever that was. Probably soup from a can.

She also noticed that her curtains were still wide open to a sky turned deep velvet. Forbidding. The only light in the room came from her computer screen and the nightlight plugged in behind a glass-top table.

Julia sprang up so fast she almost toppled her chair, a nearly impossible feat considering it was on a swivel base. Her heart raced as she flew around her house closing curtains against the darkness, checking locks on windows and doors against anything evil that lurked in the shadows...and most of all, making certain all her nightlights were burning.

Julia felt the almost-forgotten beginnings of a panic attack coming on.

She said a word she used to see on the walls of bathrooms before she moved to a town that kept everything pristine, including public toilets. Then she felt a foolish stab of guilt, as if she'd betrayed her mother. How many times had Rachel, the consummate Southern belle, reminded her that a woman who made her living stringing words together ought to have a vocabulary that would express her dismay without resorting to the mouth of a common gutter snipe.

She said it again on general principles, but also because the sound of her own voice stilled her panic. She was in the here and now, not back in the nightmare that had sent her running so hard and fast it took the edge of a continent and the Pacific Ocean to stop her. Though, practically speaking, she wasn't close enough to see the ocean without a considerable drive.

"Not today, you don't." She rubbed her forehead then took a deep breath, consciously relaxed her clenched jaw and waited.

Nothing. Good.

She made a rude gesture though nobody could possibly see, not with those blackout curtains on every window. Then she marched into her kitchen and opened a can of tomato soup. Plain. No frills. She loved cooking and she particularly loved experimenting, but tonight she was in no mood to add butter and real cream. Or maybe cream cheese with a touch of dill.

Julia ate her soup standing up, still tense, ever vigilant, turning her head toward every sound. The high-pitched voices of the nine-year-old twin boys next door, arguing with their mother about coming inside to eat. The metallic clang of a metal garbage can across her back fence. The sound of an engine, slowing as it entered the neighborhood and then stopped.

So close. Next door?

Her adrenaline surged as she crept toward the front of her house. The sound outside her door tipped her closer toward the edge of panic. Footsteps, definitely. Her friends *never* showed up without calling first. They knew better.

Had her past finally caught up with her? Was another dark horror waiting just beyond her door, taunting her that *this time* there would be no escape?

The doorbell cut through her panic. Every instinct told her to just let it ring. But what if one of her friends had an emergency?

It chimed again, and Julia headed toward her front door without even bothering to put on her shoes. Whoever was on her front porch unannounced at suppertime would have to take what they could get. Her house, her rules.

She flipped on the porch lights then glanced through the peephole - and there he stood, not a hair on his head changed from the last time she'd seen him, standing in a hotel room, begging her not to go. Five years ago. Memory probably exaggerated the begging part, but Rick had been insistent that she stay. And very persuasive.

She took a step back as if she might get scorched by the laser-look from blue eyes that, like her own, had seen too much.

He gave up on the bell and started pounding on the door. "Let me in, Julia. I know you're in there."

"How do you know?" Her reclaimed view of the peephole showed his face to be neutral, a mask that told her nothing about the enemy.

"Your mother."

Of course. Rachel would also have told him where to find her. She'd always adored Rick and would forgive him anything, much the way you would a favorite puppy that peed on the rug. Not that it would have taken any effort for him to locate her without help. After all, he *was* Special Agent Patrick Richards, FBI.

"I have nothing to say to you, Rick."

"This is not personal." He ran his hand through his hair, an old habit that separated the sprinkling of coarse gray strands and made them stand out against the black. "At least, it's not personal between us."

Rick had never lied to her. Except that one time.

"Come on, Julia. I need your help."

"You have two minutes."

She slid the chain back, unlocked the deadbolt and opened the door. A late-model burgundy Ford Explorer was parked in her driveway. He'd traded cars, then. One of the many little things she no longer knew about him.

As he strode through her hall and into her living room, a hint of Irish Spring soap drifted her way. That, she knew. And remembered all too well.

Rick catalogued every detail before he stopped in front of her stone fireplace.

"Nice." He leaned his arm against the mantle and gave her an easy smile as he nodded toward her spinet piano. "I see you left your baby grand in Chicago."

"I left lots of things in Chicago."

His expression remained neutral and his smile held. She'd forgotten how good Rick was at keeping his emotions hidden.

"Can I sit down, Julia? Or do you want me to stand here and tower over you?"

He made a point of looking at her bare feet and she almost laughed. It had been an old joke between them. She was five feet, ten inches and he was six-two. When she wore four-inch heels they were eye to eye. She'd once been fond of heels, had worked in them most of the time, even learned to run in them. She'd never given him much chance to tower. Or anybody else, for that matter.

"Sit down and start talking. Your two minutes are almost up."

He moved to the sofa and sat down beside her.

"My partner took some personal time to come to Shutter Lake. Nobody's seen or heard from him in a week."

She almost lost her soup. She totally lost her viewpoint of Rick as the enemy. When word got out that the city now had two disappearances in addition to Sylvia's murder, the shock wave of fear would turn into a tsunami.

"Julia, what's wrong? Are you sick?"

Back in Chicago Julia had perfected the art of projecting an uncompromising poker face to the world. She would never have survived the cutthroat competition of investigative journalism without it. She would never have survived the streets.

Shutter Lake had made her softer, vulnerable.

"No, I'm fine. But poor John... This is horrible." She remembered Rick's partner, a lovable round-faced guy nearing retirement.

"John retired three years ago and moved to Florida with his wife. They're happy as two clams."

"What a relief." She pushed her hair off her face. "Not that I want anybody to be missing."

"It's my current partner. Special Agent Evan Adler. A great guy with a well-developed sense of humor and a soft spot for the underdog." The photo showed a good-looking young man, probably early thirties, dark hair and eyes. "Medium build and height. About your height, Julia."

She studied it closely. Shutter Lake was no Anaheim with Disneyland but the city did get a fair share of tourists. Julia's habit of noticing details harkened back to her childhood. When she was six and gave a complete report on the new neighbors, including the black hair growing out of a wart on the man's chin, Rachel said she was obviously practicing to be director of the FBI.

"I've never seen him. But the motorcycle tours up the Pacific Coast are spectacular, and there's a big beautiful wilderness just outside my back door where mobile phone service is spotty to nonexistent." Rick was too good at his job to have raced to Shutter Lake searching for Adler without checking every other possibility first. Still, she clung to a desperate hope. "Are you sure he didn't come here to sightsee and just got out of cell phone range?"

"None of that checked out."

He'd just confirmed her worst fear.

"A lot has been going on in Shutter Lake, Rick. Things that could be relevant."

Her two-minute ultimatum abandoned, she told him everything she knew about Sylvia Cole - daughter of one of Shutter Lake's most prominent families and owner of a cleaning service named Sparkle - including the date of her murder. Rick listened with the intensity of a man storing away every detail in a photographic memory bank.

His focus never wavered as she told him about the disappearance of foreign exchange student Josie Rodriguez, glowing with pubescent beauty and so very vulnerable. She added Dana's suspicions that Josie might have been trafficked, and then told Rick about the videos Dana had heard about, which backed up her belief.

Only the slight tightening of Rick's lips when she mentioned the porn site Viva Venezuela betrayed his bone-deep hatred of anyone who preyed on the young and innocent.

"You help me find this girl, and I'll help you find Adler."

"Deal." No hesitation. No handshake. Just the firm commitment of a man who was legendary for his dogged determination and phenomenal success rate at solving the hard cases.

"Then let's get started."

He didn't say, "Now?" He didn't ask why. He knew. Time had already run out for Sylvia and was rapidly doing the same for Josie and Adler.

Chapter Two

The Rabbit Hole with its bizarre Alice-in-Wonderland look and its even more unusual color – black, inside and out, except for that ridiculous white rabbit at the door – was not Julia's favorite place to grab a beer. Too dark. Too crowded. Too likely you'd be unable to see somebody sneaking up on you. Add the creepy artificial cobwebs and giant black spiders its owner had draped outside the entrance as a nod to Halloween, and Julia felt absolutely skittish.

Not for the first time since Dana had asked her to slip backward and resurrect skills from her life in the fast lane did Julia have second thoughts. She'd come to Shutter Lake to hide in plain sight, to heal, to forget. Not to get neck deep in a crime that was becoming more twisted by the day.

"Perfect." Rick's comment jerked her out of her murky past. He'd come to a dead halt outside The Rabbit Hole, taking in everything with a sweeping glance. "This is exactly the kind of place Adler would have come."

As a matter of fact, in a small town the size of Shutter Lake it was one of the only places a young FBI agent looking to relax would go.

Rick studied her with eyes that seemed to see straight through to her soul.

"You okay?"

Julia had been taken from a bar much like The Rabbit Hole, dark, crowded and impersonal. Most people who frequented bars were not there to socialize. They'd come for liquid anesthesia and a few hours to forget.

"Why wouldn't I be?" The reply was curt, no-nonsense. It said, loud and clear, *don't you dare treat me like a broken woman because you know things about me that nobody else does.*

Nobody except her parents. And Dana. And half the world who'd followed Chicago's news five years ago.

Don't even go there.

In a show of bravado she'd honed to perfection, Julia linked arms with his. "Come on, Agent Richardson. Let's get in there while the beer is still cold and the night still young."

"This backwater town has warped you."

Maybe it saved me.

"Don't let anybody in Shutter Lake hear you call this a backwater. I'll have you know we're the best-kept secret in America. A hidden paradise."

"Says who?"

"Why do you want to know? You planning on moving here?"

"Not unless I get reassigned and sent to Hell."

Rick pushed open the door and took in the crowd. The place was jammed, and Julia didn't wonder why. Today's press conference in front of City Hall would have done nothing to tamp down the fear sweeping the town once viewed as immune to evil.

In spite of Chief of Police Griff McCabe's assurances that they were closing in on the killer, the unease among the townspeople was palpable. One of their star citizens had been murdered. Who would be next?

Not even the dead girl's parents raising their reward to two million dollars for anyone with information leading to the person who ended Sylvia's life could soothe the anxiety of people reeling with shock. It was no wonder they'd packed into The Rabbit Hole. They were looking for the din of voices to drown out fear and the proximity of neighbors alive with liquid courage to restore their sense of security.

The decibel level went up with Julia and Rick's arrival. Speculation about the new man in town, no doubt. Small towns were that way.

As they wove through the crowd toward the bar, she scanned the masses for familiar faces. It was not yet the weekend, and it was past closing time for most of the downtown shops. Two of the shops' owners sat on barstools nursing drinks. One was Nolan Ikard, owner and barista of the The Grind, a shop so good it could have held its own anywhere in the country. The slump of his shoulders and the way he was staring into his beer said he was alone and not looking for chatter.

Two stools down from him was Heidi Udall, her ample hips spilling over the stool, proof that she was her own best customer at Batter Up, the bakery famous in town for a variety of cupcakes and other sweet treats guaranteed to break even the most staunch health nut's diet. Even sitting still, she was in perpetual motion, darting furtive glances around the room, her face both expectant and brooding, as if she were looking for somebody but wasn't quite sure whether she wanted to see them.

Heidi's gaze lit on Julia, but she quickly turned her head away, pretending she didn't see her. What was up with that? She'd never done a thing to Heidi Udall except show a preference for the bagels at The Grind to the calorie-laden confections Heidi served.

Maybe Julia was reading motives that weren't there. Maybe Heidi was reacting to Rick. She wasn't the most socially adept woman in Shutter Lake. In fact, a fairly reliable grapevine had it that Heidi had never had a relationship that lasted beyond the first date. Rick's excessive good looks had sent women more sophisticated than the town's baker into a swoon. It was comical, really, their reaction to him.

Suddenly Julia's senses went on full alert. She felt the stare as if hands had brushed across her neck and down her arms. Following her instinct, she glanced into the dark corner on the far side of the bar. Griff McCabe sat with his back to the wall and his face to the front door, making no bones about checking her out, trying to fathom what she was up to.

Or maybe it was Julia's own conscience that read motives into his frank assessment of her and her unexpected date for the evening. She was treading into somebody else's territory. Missing persons was the responsibility of McCabe and his police department, specifically his deputy chief, Laney Holt, whose acerbic wit and independent nature had made her gravitate toward Julia when Laney had moved to Shutter Lake. Two years ago. It seemed they'd been friends forever.

Laney sat beside McCabe wearing an expression that was half-amused, half-questioning. She quirked an eyebrow at the sight of the man with his hand still on Julia's back, and then she winked. She'd give Julia the third degree about Rick at their next girls' night out. She and Dana both.

Though both her friends would endure splinters under their nails before talking about Julia's business, nobody else quaffing beers here tonight would be bound by such loyalty. By tomorrow word would be all over town that "The Good Life" columnist down at the *Firefly* was at The Rabbit Hole having a high-heel time of her own.

Such was life in a small town. Talk about the lives of others kept you from having to think about the sorry state of your own. Or the fabulous state, whichever applied.

"Two people are leaving." Rick pressed her forward and they slid onto stools vacated by Nolan and a middle-aged hippie-type Julia didn't recognize. Probably one of the organic farmers who sold the freshest fruits and vegetables this side of heaven at the open-air market on the west side of town.

She slid onto the bar stool next to Heidi and Rick took the one on her left.

"Hi, Heidi!" The devil made Julia use her mother's overly jovial social maven voice. She'd find out what was eating the baker in two minutes flat.

Heidi's response to Julia was unenthusiastic. But her interest in Rick was so avid her cheeks rouged.

Julia made the introductions and Rick gave her a look that said *what's up with that?* Fine. Heidi's current bad mood wasn't worth her time. She was here for more than frivolous conversation.

The guy approaching was just the man she wanted to see.

Ray Jones, bartender and owner, hustled her way, appealing smile firmly in place. He knew he was easy on the eyes and he used it to full advantage. Under pretense of giving the bar a swipe, he leaned in close enough for her to smell the peppermint candies on his breath. He kept them in open dishes throughout The Rabbit Hole.

"Nice perfume, Julia." Ray would flirt with a fencepost. Granted, she had a few more curves, but she also had more than ten years on him. "What's it called?"

"Poison. You planning on buying some, Ray?"

That cooled his cucumber.

Rick didn't so much lean between them as loom. "Two beers. Guinness here and a Michelob draft for Julia." Ray hurried off, all business now, and the noise in the bar settled down to a low roar. "You still drink that?"

"I do. But if you'd said 'one for the lady' I'd have socked you."

"More likely, laid a round-house kick on me. Don't worry, Julia. I know better than to mess with you."

"See that you keep it that way."

Ray was back, and Rick wasted no time in pulling out a photo of Adler.

"I'm looking for this man. He was in Shutter Lake about a

week ago, and I have reason to believe he was here."

"I can't keep up with everybody who comes here."

"Take a closer look." Rick flashed his badge and slid the photo across the bar. "He's Special Agent Evan Adler. The FBI takes a personal interest in the whereabouts of their own."

Something flickered in Ray's eyes, a look Julia recognized when the person being questioned was shutting down and planned to be evasive. Or outright lie. Was it any wonder he was skittish? With murder in the wind and a killer on the loose, people didn't know whether telling what they knew would make them a witness, a suspect or a victim.

"Ray, this is just a friendly visit." Julia didn't feel the slightest twinge about widening her eyes and giving her voice a hint of feminine promise. She'd been trained by the best – her mother. And she'd long ago learned that flattery can loosen the tongue and derail lies. "You've got one of the best memories in town. It would really help if you could remember whether you saw him."

"Yeah, I saw him." Ray addressed his remarks to Julia. "He was in here. I don't recall exactly when. I'm no Einstein."

"It doesn't have to be exact. An estimate will do."

"It was probably about a week ago."

"Thanks, Ray." Beside her, Rick seemed content to let her keep the lead. "Was Adler with anybody?"

"That, I remember for sure. Who could miss her?" Ray went quiet. Whatever memories he'd dredged up misted his eyes.

Years ago she'd learned the art of silence from her mentor at *Chicago World,* a seasoned balding reporter with more awards than hair on his head. *Julia, sometimes you can find out more by listening than by asking.*

Leaning closer to Ray so her body language telegraphed sympathy, she waited and listened.

Finally he cleared his throat. "It was Sylvia Cole."

Julia's instincts went on full alert and she could feel the tension rolling off Rick. She didn't dare look at him.

"Sylvia was with Adler?"

"Yeah, Julia, that's what I said."

"Did you happen to overhear them?"

"I don't make a practice of eavesdropping on my customers. You ought to know that."

"I know you don't, Ray, but Adler is FBI. And Sylvia is dead."

As Julia let the reminders sink in, she watched the owner/bartender.

He polished the bar in front of them, rubbing at stains that weren't there. Finally he looped the bar rag into his belt and faced her. Eyes level. No pretense.

"I see and hear a lot in The Rabbit Hole. If I had heard anything at all that might help catch the person who killed Sylvia, I'd have already told Chief McCabe or Deputy Holt."

He nodded in the direction of their booth. Laney Holt appeared to be calmly drinking her beer. She was always hard to read. But Julia could tell by the way she observed that Laney wasn't missing a bit of the exchange with Ray at the bar.

On the other hand, the Chief of Police had his jaw clenched and Rick firmly in his sights. Easy to read that body language. *You're treading on my turf.*

Julia turned her attention back to the bartender. "I know you would have, Ray. Just as I know you'd tell us if you heard anything that could shed any light on why Agent Adler was with Sylvia."

"I would. And I didn't."

Satisfied Ray was telling the truth Julia relaxed, her body language a signal she was done.

Rick pocketed the photo and took the reins. "Adler was driving a black SUV. A last year's model Jeep Grand Cherokee. Did you happen to see it?"

"No. I rarely see what anybody's driving unless I'm out back taking a break. Not much parking around the bar. Most of my customers end up using that big parking lot by the church across the street." Ray turned back to Julia. "Anything else I can do for you? I've got a full house tonight."

"Thanks. You've been a big help… Oh, one more thing." She passed a photo of Josie to him. "Did you ever see this girl in here?"

Ray studied the photo then flipped it back to her. "You know I don't let underage kids in here, Julia."

"I know that, Ray, but she worked part-time with Sylvia. I thought maybe she tarted herself up and sneaked in with her boss after work."

"Sylvia wouldn't have allowed that. She protected her employees like a hawk. Everybody in town knew that."

"Guess I missed it. Thanks again, Ray."

Before Rick could get his billfold out of his pocket, Julia paid for her own beer then marched off with his what's-up-with-that look boring into her back. The second of the evening.

She didn't care. She'd made good her promise to help. Anything else was off the table. Friendship. Memories. A resurrected affair. Her entire past.

Rick caught up with her, but he didn't take her arm. Didn't put his hand on her back. She did allow him to open the door. Rachel's doing. Drat those infernal Southern manners.

They stood a few feet apart, breathing the night air. The temperature had dropped considerably since they'd gone into The Rabbit Hole. Night air sweeping into the valley from the Sierras. Julia wished she'd worn a heavier sweater. Truth be told, she wished for her bed, a glass of chardonnay and a good book. She wished for anything except standing in downtown Shutter Lake with a man from her past.

"Adler was with your murder victim, Julia."

"Sylvia Cole's not *my* murder victim. I no longer cover crime."

"I forgot. You cover small town fundraisers and little old ladies' church circles."

"Sarcasm always did become you, Agent Richardson."

"You, too, Pulitzer-Prize winner Ford."

They stared at each other, their postures stiff. Finally Julia began to feel ridiculous.

"I never won the Pulitzer." She was nominated – and had won a host of awards – but not the big one. For a moment the old itch to nab the Pulitzer came back.

"You should have." His face softened. "You were that good."

"I should say thank you."

"Why don't you?"

"Okay. Thanks, Rick." He flashed his heart-stopping smile. Thanks to time and space and a steel backbone, her heart kept on beating. "But that doesn't mean you'll be sleeping in my guest room."

"I never thought I would."

"Good. We've settled that."

"Not entirely."

Whatever Rick meant by that, Julia didn't want to know. Or perhaps she just chose to ignore it. She'd been down one rabbit hole tonight. She wasn't about to go down another.

"So where does one stay in beautiful downtown Shutter

Lake?"

"One? Beautiful downtown? You're slipping, Rick. You're usually more scathing than that."

"Back to the insults, are we?"

"Well, no." She raked her hand through her mane of hair, made herself take some deep breaths. "Follow me."

"Any time, anywhere."

Instead of rising to his bait, Julia lengthened her stride so he had to hustle. Here's a woman in charge, her pace said. Here's a woman who refuses to be dragged backward.

She cut through the town's square. No threats here, even at night. Ornate street lights illuminated the cobblestone pathways and the fountain in the center of the park. Water spilling from the Italian-inspired cherubs and dolphins caught the light and were transformed into a magical display that took Julia's breath.

Before she'd come to Shutter Lake she hadn't had enough free time to truly appreciate beauty, natural or otherwise. Total commitment to her job robbed her of leisurely outings to Chicago's great museums and architectural monuments to the genius of Frank Lloyd Wright. She'd made a few whirlwind trips, but nothing that would allow her to linger in front of Picasso or enjoy a picnic lunch on the lake while she marveled over Chicago's skyline. Her adopted home had given her that time, and she was grateful.

As they moved beyond the fountain, she noticed the stage for Saturday's concert and fundraiser had already been set up. Across the street, Windermere Center for the Arts loomed in the dark.

Rick was quiet, a signal he was taking in every detail, including the temporary nature of the stage. But if he noticed the beauty of the square at night he didn't mention it. Not surprising. He was practical to the bone.

"So, where are we headed?"

They'd come to the north side of the square beyond the reach of bright lights. Julia stood in a patch of shadow that could hide expressions, intentions, and even evil. She suppressed a shiver.

"Just across the street. The B&B on Main. We'll check you in then go back to my house for your clothes and your car."

"Works for me."

The B&B on Main was a two-story Victorian house so impressive in size it could hold its own with Windermere Center for the Arts next door. But size is where they parted company.

While the arts center was imposing and elegant with Corinthian columns lining the front and beveled glass in every window, the B&B sported an outrageous pink exterior with bright aquamarine gingerbread trim. A few snobbish citizens described it as gaudy. In the daylight you could spot it anywhere on the square which had been the exact intent of the owner, who was no stranger to flamboyance.

Julia and Rick climbed painted wooden steps flanked by glowing plastic jack o' lanterns to a porch lit with Victorian lamps. It was filled with deep-cushioned wicker rockers and white wicker plant stands that held ferns beginning to show the effects of nights that were too cold for potted greenery. Both porch floor and ceiling were painted a lighter shade of blue. Julia didn't know if the intent was to soothe or to honor the old myth that blue drove off *haints,* a term only heard in a few pockets of the Deep South.

This town could stand a little of both - soothing plus getting rid of the ghosts resurrected by murder and haunting every corner of Shutter Lake.

She punched the bell beside a massive ornately carved front door. The etched glass panels featured horses, a sure sign the house had not stood on this corner across from Johnny's on Main for more than a hundred years. In fact it had been built twenty years ago by the woman who came to the door.

Brenda Lockhart. As outrageous as the colors on her house.

"Well, look what the cat dragged in!" she said. "Julia Ford!"

Brenda stood barely above five feet, even in her red cowboy boots. Her pink western-style shirt dripped with fringe that only served to emphasize her generous bust. She'd topped off her outfit with a red cowboy hat balanced on a mop of gray curls that looked like Kentucky kudzu growing wild. Though it was well past ten, the seventy-year-old native Kentuckian looked as fresh as anybody half her age.

"Brenda, this is Patrick Richardson...Rick, Brenda Lockhart, owner of the B&B."

"And chief cook, bottle washer and every other thing that goes on around here." She flung open the door. "Come on in and make yourself at home. I don't get many as handsome as you. You a movie star?"

"I'm afraid not."

"Damn good thing, I'd say."

The inside of the B&B was even more surprising than the outside. No velvet Victorian sofas and fringed curtains here. Brenda had decorated in what she called Early Cowboy, top to bottom – heavy brass and wrought iron chandeliers, wide sofas upholstered in earth tones and built for comfort, oversized oak side tables, lamps with polished horn bases.

A genuine Frederic Remington masterwork hung behind the massive oak check-in counter, a Native American on a pony, untitled. Occasionally you'd find a blank spot on the wall when Brenda loaned the painting to an art museum.

If you asked her about the painting, she'd tell you she came from a horseracing family and had more money than God. The walls in every room of the B&B were covered with photographs of winning race horses she'd bred in her native state for thirty years before she lost her husband.

A couple of years back, Julia had done a feature on Brenda Lockhart. When her husband died, she'd bought a ranch off Old Mine Road south of town and settled in with a stable of thoroughbred horses. It was her horses that won Brenda easy acceptance by Shutter Lake's wealthiest residents.

Ignoring the computer on her check-in counter, Brenda pulled out an old fashioned ledger to record Rick's information. She was known for her distrust of technology. She didn't have a web page and never advertised online. She rarely even put an ad in print media. Word of mouth was good enough for her, she always said. It was a miracle anybody ever found her.

She hated technology so much she sometimes wouldn't even answer her phone. That would explain why Julia very seldom saw guests at the bed and breakfast inn. In fact, she suspected Brenda had built the place in the city for herself and then got lonesome without her horses and decided to turn it into a bed and breakfast inn.

There was a strong possibility Evan Adler had stayed here since it served as Shutter Lake's only hotel. Julia was glad to see that Rick didn't ask. You don't barge in on a woman her age late at night and start quizzing her.

"You're my only guest except a honey-mooning couple from Las Vegas. You won't be seeing much of them. Or me, either, 'til morning."

"Works for me."

"Good. You look like a man who can take care of himself. Soon as I check you in, I'm headed up to bed. But I'll see you in morning. Breakfast is at six. That suit you?"

"It does."

"Rick, we're going to get along just fine. I like a man who knows how to get up with the sun and start the day. Shows character." She handed him a key. "This goes to the front door, in case you need to leave and come back while I'm getting my beauty sleep. There are no room keys. There never was any reason to lock your bedroom door 'til Sylvia Cole got murdered."

Rick showed no reaction as he pocketed the key. "I'm headed out to get my bags. It's good to know I can get in without having to disturb you. Thank you, Mrs. Lockhart."

"Shoot, Mr. Lockhart's been dead so long I barely even remember what he looked like. Call me Brenda. Everybody else does."

After they'd checked in and said goodnight to Brenda, they walked back to Julia's house. She was glad Rick didn't comment that every house on Harmony Street had jack o' lanterns glowing in their entrance. Every house except hers.

He knew her last story for *Chicago World* had been about the Jack o' Lantern serial killer. But he had sense enough not to bring it up.

Julia averted her eyes from the carved pumpkins, dismayed they still had the power to undo her. Each October she hoped her serene years in Shutter Lake had rid her of that Achilles heel... and each Halloween whispered to her *not yet.*

Rick walked her all the way to the door, too, knowing she had an independent streak a mile wide. It didn't take an FBI agent to understand that she was as spooked by Sylvia's murder as everyone else in town. And though Rick was one of the few who knew her anxiety went far deeper, he didn't offer any false comfort.

"I'd ask you in for coffee, but it's late. We can regroup in the morning."

"Early in the morning." Rick chuckled. "Looks like I'll be up at six."

"Don't expect me then. Early bird is not my style."

The look he gave her said, *I know.* "I'll pick you up. We might need the car."

"Eight."

"Done."

He watched until she was inside. Fine. Crime was collecting in Shutter Lake like pollen in spring. Julia went straight to her shower to scrub it off her skin. Then she wrapped herself in a white terrycloth robe and padded barefoot to her kitchen.

No need to turn on overhead lights. Her multitude of nightlights provided a well-lit pathway throughout the house. She went straight to her refrigerator, got a bottle of chardonnay from Alexander Valley Vineyards in Sonoma County then stood there balancing one foot on the other. She could almost taste the cool liquid, almost feel the tension easing out of her body.

"Not tonight, Jack."

She put the bottle back into the refrigerator then went into her bedroom and lay down under her sheets.

"You can do this. You can go to sleep."

Her nightlight cast shadows that danced along the blue walls while her mind raced with possibilities, leads to explore, connections. Three times she cast aside her sheet with the intention of powering up her computer for research. She tossed the covers back a fourth time with the idea that she was dying of thirst and one glass of chardonnay wouldn't hurt.

Finally, Julia willed herself to lie still. Even if she couldn't fall asleep, at least she could get some rest.

Chapter Three

Friday, October 12

"You look like hell."

Holt stood in Griff's doorway looking as if she'd been pressed at the local laundry then spit out clean and creased. He, on the other hand, looked exactly like the hell she'd pinned on him.

He didn't have to glance in the mirror to know what Holt saw after she'd rousted him out of bed at oh-God o'clock. Eyes bleary from drink. Beard stubble rough as sandpaper. Rumpled boxers - clean, thank God - and a tee shirt that hadn't been near a washing machine in he couldn't remember when. Hair sticking up like some gooney bird.

"Thank you, Deputy Chief Holt." He flung open his door. "Come on in and make some coffee. You know where the pot is."

"What am I? Your servant?"

He just grunted and left her to find her way to the kitchen. She didn't require a reply. Holt pulled his chain on principle. And he put up with it for too many reasons to count. For one, he needed her to catch Sylvia's killer. She was a good cop, a damned good one, and if he didn't have Laney's big city instincts and expertise on this case, his whole town would be rioting by now.

"Make it snappy, Chief," she called after him.

"Yeah, yeah."

He slid out of his shorts and tee shirt and saw a bruise on his hip that hadn't been there the day before. Did he fall last night? Bump into furniture? He couldn't remember, and that scared him.

He downed the flash of anxiety with a quick shower followed by eye drops, a scrub with toothbrush and a swish of mouthwash. Afterward McCabe felt halfway human. By the time he'd donned jeans and one of the white shirts the laundry kept spic and span, he made a good imitation of a man ready to take on murder.

What a joke. He'd do well to take on the cup of coffee his deputy had waiting for him in the kitchen.

He nabbed the cup and straddled a bar stool.

"What's up, Holt?"

"We got a DNA match from Sylvia's sheets and the tooth brush in her bathroom."

"And?"

"It's Ikard's."

"How in the hell did you get Ikard's DNA?"

"Dana watch-dogged his fork and napkin down at Stacked 'til I could bag them."

He held up his hand. "Wait a minute. I don't want to know."

"It was trash, McCabe. He abandoned it."

"I still don't want to know."

"Well, I guess Ikard went on Geneology.com and they got it. That suit you, Chief?"

"Nothing about this case suits me." He shoved aside his coffee cup. "Let's go find out what Ikard's got to say."

"I'm driving."

"I'm not arguing." He nabbed his leather jacket and followed her out the door.

His ranch style house was too far outside the city limits to walk to The Grind, but the long hike might have done Griff some good, got some oxygen circulating in his blood instead of all that alcohol. He'd topped off an evening of beers at The Rabbit Hole with a Jack Daniels. Or two. Maybe more. Who was counting?

He was glad to sink into the passenger side of Holt's SUV and let her do the driving. It gave him a few more minutes to clear his head. The Sylvia Cole case was a nightmare. With the kid Vinn Bradshaw being cleared of murder, that sick pervert Wade Travis not panning out and Zion Cole raising Cain because his daughter's killer was still on the loose, McCabe was scrambling to keep the police department – himself in particular – from looking incompetent.

The trip to downtown Shutter Lake didn't take as long as McCabe needed to get his shit together. His mood got even worse when Holt parked behind a maroon Ford Explorer with out-of-state license plates. The SUV had FBI written all over it. Probably the man who was sticking his nose into McCabe's business at The Rabbit Hole last night.

He'd had too many beers to ask, but it took Holt only a minute to dig the truth out of Ray. FBI Special Agent Evan Adler was missing, last seen in Shutter Lake and not heard from since. As if they needed another reason for everybody in this town to go crazy.

If they didn't catch Sylvia's killer soon, he was liable to have a riot on his hands. It was happening all over the bigger cities in this screwed-up country. Who knew when a respectable little town like Shutter Lake would become a powder keg? And how little it would take to make it one.

He pushed open the door to The Grind.

There was Julia Ford sitting in the corner with the FBI, their heads together, two cups of coffee - plain it appeared - on the table between them. McCabe's gut twisted.

First, she shows up at The Rabbit Hole with him and now here. What was Ford trying to do? Work herself back into the big time? Mess around in his case and get the scoop that would land her at FOX? Or maybe her politics leaned the other way. Maybe she wanted to end up anchoring prime time news at CNN.

"Ikard's not here." Holt's voice jerked him back to the business at hand.

A quick survey of the coffee shop showed it empty of customers except the two who got under his skin. It was still too early for the work crowd. That was probably why Holt had dragged him out of bed at an indecent hour. Both of them preferred to work without an audience.

Suddenly a word from Julia's soft flow of conversation leaped out at him. *Trafficked.* What the hell? Trafficked as in human trafficking? That fell under federal jurisdiction, and if it happened in his town, McCabe would be the first one they contacted.

He was Shutter Lake though and through. Born here before the city was even incorporated. Raised here. And now trying to keep the peace and catch a killer here. This was his town. If the Feds didn't bother notifying him of trafficking and were instead hooking up with that former hotshot investigative reporter to mess around in his case, heads would roll.

"McCabe? You with me?" Holt gave him a look that said *Get it together.*

"Yeah." He swung his gaze toward Shonda Reed, Ikard's assistant, college kid with a whole lot of funny-colored hair. Strawberry blond, he thought it was called. His ex-wife had tried for that color once. It turned her hair green.

Shonda was standing behind the counter looking like she'd seen her worst enemy.

"I'll talk to her," Holt said. She had an uncanny knack for knowing when he needed her to take the lead.

"Wait a sec. Maybe Ikard's in the back."

"Maybe he's still in bed. You want me to trot upstairs and rattle his chain?"

"Don't mess with me, Holt."

Nolan Ikard lived in an apartment above The Grind. Though he had made a huge success of his coffee shop, this wouldn't be the first time he'd opened up and left Shonda in charge. He was, after all, the type ladies fell for. Tall and lean with light hair and eyes. He probably kept late hours.

He was also young. Thirty. No record. No reason to kill Sylvia that they knew of. Yet.

"Time's wasting, Chief."

As if he didn't know that. "Okay. I'll grab bagels and coffee. You do the talking. "

"Deal."

McCabe didn't even bother looking at the menu. All those fancy names for coffee with ten pounds of sugar and fat added to enhance the flavor. It did nothing but ruin a perfectly good cup of joe. He liked his coffee black, plain and uncomplicated.

He placed the order, got two coffees in go cups and a bag of bagels then stepped back to watch Holt in action. Maybe he could learn a few things from her. One more secret he planned to keep to himself.

Holt wasn't ego-driven like a lot of people in this town, but he didn't want her getting the big head and leaving Shutter Lake for some larger city where she'd make headlines. Of the right kind. The cop-catches-killer kind.

If he didn't get a break soon, he'd have some headlines of his own. *McCabe, Incompetent Closet Alcoholic, Lets Killer Slip Through His Fingers.*

"'Morning, Shonda," Holt said.

"Oh…" The young woman got that deer-in-the-headlights look of somebody cornered. And Holt hadn't even started on her yet. "Hi."

McCabe eased back a few steps and leaned against the counter, far enough from Holt so he wouldn't further spook Shonda but close enough to the corner table so he could hear what Ford and the FBI were up to. If he got lucky.

They were keeping their voices low. *Smart.* No sense going around broadcasting business. Especially if it was none of your business.

"Is Ikard here?"

"No." Shonda cast a furtive glance around the shop as if her boss might be hiding behind one of the espresso machines or lurking under one of the tables.

"Too bad." Holt was keeping it loose and casual, a style that until Sylvia's murder had suited McCabe's mood. "Has the boss been in this morning?"

"He opened up." Shonda twisted the dish cloth in her hands. "Then he left."

"Do you know where he was going?"

"He didn't say."

"Did he say when he'd be back?"

"No."

"Let's think about this a while, Shonda. Maybe he named his destination and told you when he'd return but you were so busy you didn't pay close attention. That happens to me sometimes. And I'm trained to pay attention."

The young woman's shoulders relaxed a bit, but she kept a tight grip on her washcloth. What else was she keeping a tight grip on? Her boss's secrets?

"No, he didn't mention his plans."

"You're sure about that?"

Holt waited a beat, giving the girl time to wonder what kind of trouble she might get into for lying to the law. McCabe had seen that tactic work for his deputy numerous times.

"I'm sure."

Everything about Holt's posture said she was done here. McCabe tossed the coffee he'd hardly touched and closed in on the nervous barista.

"Shonda, I hope you don't mind a few more questions."

She fidgeted in a way that could imply guilt but more likely implied that she was scared whatever she said would either piss off the Chief of Police or her boss.

He gave her time to let his size and authority sink in. He hated that, using intimidation tactics. Especially on a young woman who probably didn't have a thing to do with Sylvia Cole's murder. Still, everybody was breathing down his back. Sylvia's daddy, Zion Cole. Thomas Jessup, the mayor. Even poor, broken-hearted Yolanda Cole, who just wanted to bury her daughter.

The bells over the front door tinkled and a rush of up-and-coming yuppie types hurried inside yakking about everything from the weather – beautiful – to their jobs – very promising. When they saw the Chief of Police had pretty little Shonda cowering like a rabbit, their conversation stalled.

Well, hell. He hated everything about this case. Having half the town looking over his shoulder while he hunted a killer. Standing in The Grind trying to track down a suspect so his department would look like they were doing their job.

DNA on the sheets didn't mean you'd committed murder, but right now it was the best lead he had.

Holt quirked an eyebrow at him and crossed her arms over her chest, body language that said she was anxious to move on.

"Tell you what, Shonda, I'm not going to waste your time and I don't want you wasting mine." He shot a look at his deputy. "Holt, give her your card."

He didn't miss the tremble in Shonda's hand when she took it.

"I want you to think long and hard about where your boss is and what you might have said that we could construe as obstructing justice. When you come up with something, you call this number. Have I made myself clear?"

"Yes."

Why didn't young people ever say "sir" and "ma'am" anymore? As a matter of fact, hardly anybody in Shutter Lake used those terms except Griff. It showed respect, common courtesy. And maybe it showed he was getting old. At forty, wouldn't that be a hell of a note?

As he and Holt left he shot one last glance in Ford's direction. Was she still nosing around in his case? Or had she sniffed out his dirty secret? He knew she'd once been good enough. She'd been a well-known award-winning journalist in one of the big Chicago papers. There'd been quite a stir down at the *Firefly* when they landed her.

When she first came here, Griff had thought she'd do important pieces. He'd been looking forward to some intelligent commentary about politics and big issues facing Shutter Lake as well as the rest of the country. Failing water supply. Unprincipled destruction of natural resources. Pollution of everything from mountain streams to rivers and oceans. It took him by surprise that one of the best investigative journalists in the country wrote about antiques and church suppers.

The biggest story she'd covered since coming to Shutter Lake was on the owner of the B&B on Main, Brenda Lockhart. She'd brought horses from Kentucky that were descended from Seabiscuit. Griff had bought two of them. Magnificent animals.

He'd give a month's pay to be home riding one now instead of looking for Nolan Ikard.

The minute they were outside, Holt cornered him.

"Obstructing justice? Are you out of your mind? Shonda didn't even come close."

"We know that but she doesn't. I thought it might scare her enough to give up Ikard's whereabouts."

"Do you think he skipped town?"

"You tell me, Holt. You're the one with the creds."

"What's eating you? That limp you've got that I'm not even going to mention?"

"Good. Don't."

"Fine. Let's head next door to Batter Up and see what Heidi Udall knows about Ikard."

"Plenty. She keeps tabs on him like the Gestapo." They strode across the alley with his hip complaining at every step. "This had better be good."

"Hip bothering you?"

"I thought you weren't going to mention it. And the answer is no."

"Maybe we ought to swing by the clinic after we leave here and let Ana check it out."

Holt's friend Dr. Ana Perez was good-looking, efficient, brilliant. Though she was something of a loner and a bit of a mystery, Shutter Lake was lucky to have her. But he'd be damned if he'd see her about his hip. The first thing she'd want to know is how he injured it. He didn't have a clue. And wouldn't that make him look like a fool?

"Are you hard of hearing, Holt? I said no."

"Fine, then. Let's see what Heidi knows."

~

Nothing, it turned out.

Holt had kept the baker stewing and fuming and denying for ten minutes. Heidi usually had her nose in everybody's business. And if she popped up with one more stupid question at one of Griff's press conferences, he was liable to arrest her just on general principles. Today she was suddenly acting like a Sphinx.

Holt had finally given up and walked out.

The minute they were out the door, Holt said, "Heidi's lying."

"Maybe that spooky-looking girl who occasionally helps her knows something. What's her name? Shenandoah Orange Juice?"

Holt shot him a nasty look. Apparently she was in no mood for humor, particularly his brand.

"Sheena Appleton. It's doubtful she knows anything. She spends most of her time at the bakery in Grass Valley. And for your information, she's not spooky."

"Hell, she's got blue hair and never wears a thing except black."

"That's a fashion statement, not a flaw." Holt tightened her jaw then fired up the engine and shot off like she was trying to win a NASCAR race. What was eating her? He was supposed to be the one unraveling in the face of unsolved murder.

"Better slow down. You'll get a ticket."

"Who's planning to give it? The law's sitting in my car."

His only response was a grunt.

Holt reached into the bag on the seat between them and dug out a bagel. When her phone lit up, she glanced at the screen and mouthed *Zion Cole.*

Well, hell. The grieving father, and McCabe with Jack shit. Just one more reason to ruin his day.

Chapter Four

Griff McCabe had rattled Shonda.

Julia sat at her table in The Grind long after the Chief of Police and Laney left and the yuppie crowd had grabbed their morning brew and rushed off to their jobs. Maybe the relative quiet would calm Shonda's nerves. Relaxed people were far easier to interview than those who were scared.

Finally, Julia shoved her half-empty cup aside. "You stay here, and I'll ask the questions. One more lawman in her face is liable to send her into hysteria."

Rick nodded and she strolled casually toward the young barista.

"Hi, Shonda. You've got a nice selection of bagels this morning."

"You want one?"

"I'll have one of the dill cream cheese and one raspberry cream cheese." If Rick had lost his sweet tooth he'd have to make do. "To go, please."

Shonda busied herself filling the order. When she came back to Julia, some of the high color had left her face and she seemed more in charge of her own emotions.

Obviously Laney and McCabe had been here about the murder case. Julia was shocked when she felt the stirrings of old urges. The desire to know, to be in the thick of crime and chasing down leads.

She hoped it was a signal she was beginning to put Halloween behind her.

"Shonda, did you ever see Josie Rodriguez in here?"

"All the time. Raspberry Chai was her favorite drink."

"When did you last see her?"

"I don't know. I can't keep up with dates and times and stuff like that."

"Do you recall if you ever saw her in here with anybody else?"

"Sylvia is the only one I remember. She was so beautiful, who could miss her? She was sweet, too. Always very nice to me. Josie worked at Sparkle part-time and sort of idolized her boss."

"Thanks, Shonda." Julia laid the photo of Evan Adler on the counter. "What about this man? Have you ever seen him?"

Shonda's eyes narrowed and her forehead glistened with nervous sweat.

"Wait a minute. You used to be somebody big back in Chicago. Are you doing some kind of story?"

Though it had been Julia's choice to leave her former high-powered position, she was slightly rattled at being called a has-been. She told herself to consider the source. Shonda was a student over at Sierra College, probably no more than nineteen or twenty.

"No, I'm just asking a few questions for friends. And I hope you have some answers." Julia put on a party smile, compliments of her mother. She could almost hear Rachel saying, *Julia, emotions are best kept at home. Always show a party face to the public.*

"If you *are* doing a story and just want to keep it on the QT, be sure to spell my name right. It's S-H-O-N-D-A. Hardly anybody gets it right."

"If I were doing a story, I'd be sure to get it right." She tapped the photo. "Now, about this man…"

"If he's not a regular, I wouldn't know him. Honest. And I don't pay attention to strangers off the street. It's none of my business who comes in here."

"The guy's name is Evan Adler. He's about thirty, I'd say." Julia purposely left off his profession.

"Is he new in town?"

"No, he was here visiting."

"I don't remember faces." Shonda chewed her bottom lip. "We get tourists in here all the time. I can't keep up with everybody. Nolan's the one keeps up with the customers."

Every one of Julia's instincts said the girl was lying.

"Hmm…It's odd you've never seen him."

"What do you mean?"

"Evan's a Chicago man, very fond of bagels." Julia invented as she talked. "He knew before he came to Shutter Lake that The Grind makes the best bagels in California. I can almost guarantee he was in here." She slid the photo an inch closer, and Shonda picked it up to stare. "Does that ring any bells now?"

"Now that I think of it, I believe he might have been here."

"Was he alone?"

"No. You see…that's why I finally thought of it. A man who

looked similar to that picture came in with Sylvia."

Julia tamped down an excitement that bordered on alarm. A quick glance in the mirror behind the coffee bar assured her it didn't show.

"Did they talk to you or Nolan?"

"No. I don't think they talked to anybody. Nolan waited on them but they seemed in a hurry." Shonda's cheeks began to redden, and she fidgeted with a display of gourmet chocolates near the cash register.

"You're doing great, Shonda. And you're very helpful. It's really important to my friend that we find this man. Especially after what happened to poor Sylvia."

"Did he kill her?"

Oh, my God!

"No, of course not."

But what if he had? Plenty of good lawmen had gone bad. Their advantages over other criminals were the badges that made them appear safe and an expertise that made them almost impossible to catch.

Surely Rick would have suspected, even if his suspicions amounted to nothing more than a gut feeling. If he had, though, he would have told her.

Or would he?

"Shonda, one more thing. When Sylvia left with Adler, were they walking or driving?"

"I don't know. It's always too busy in The Grind for me to look out the window. I barely have time for a bathroom break, especially if Nolan's not here."

He'd been absent all morning. It wasn't like him to leave his shop entirely in the hands of Shonda. She was competent but she didn't have the same stakes in The Grind as the owner.

"Where is he?"

"Like I told Chief McCabe. I don't know."

"Thank you, Shonda. You've been very helpful."

Julia signaled to Rick with a nod toward the door then headed out of The Grind and across the street to the town square. The park's west side faced the coffee shop and held an inviting display of shaded picnic tables and benches.

She sat down on a bench out of the sightline to The Grind. Though Shonda claimed she had no time to see anything out the window, Julia sensed she hadn't been telling the whole truth. But which part of her story was a lie?

"What's the hurry, Julia?" She shrugged her shoulders and Rick slid onto the bench across the table then accepted the raspberry cream cheese bagel she pulled out of the bag. "I've already had breakfast."

"I know."

"A substantial one. Biscuits as big as cat heads. I had to eat two to please Brenda." He took a bite of the bagel and made a sound of satisfaction. "You remembered."

"Don't make anything of it."

"I'm not."

"Good... Rick, I've got a bone to pick with you."

"This sounds serious."

"Dead serious." Her appetite for food gone, Julia put the bagel she'd nibbled on back into the bag. "Do you think Evan Adler might have murdered Sylvia Cole?"

"Are you out of your mind!" The man who always kept his cool was suddenly struggling to keep a rein on his temper.

"I don't know. Ray saw him with Sylvia and so did Shonda, so you tell me."

"That's flimsy evidence to label a man a killer."

"I'm not pinning a label on him. But don't you think it's odd that the two of them were spotted together at least twice about the time Sylvia was murdered. And then Adler disappeared. That's not coincidence, Rick."

"Are you saying Adler killed Sylvia and ran?"

"No. I'm asking you if he *could* have. Is it possible Special Agent Evan Adler had seen more cruelty on the job than he could handle? He was young. Agents have snapped before."

"I know that."

One minute Rick was on the picnic bench chewing his bagel and the next he'd vanished inside himself where nobody could get in. Not even Julia, whom he'd once claimed to love.

She retrieved her bagel from the bag, took a small bite then wrapped it back in the napkin and waited. The sun was climbing and the day was growing warm. She took off her blue cardigan and tied it around her neck.

"That sweater matches your eyes."

She wasn't about to go down that road again with Rick. "So,

what did you decide? Is Adler capable of murder?"

"No."

"Is that unequivocal?"

"Yes." Rick leaned his elbows on the picnic table. "Listen, Julia. You didn't know him the way I did. He was the kind of man who would stop to rescue a sack of kittens tossed to the side of the road. Once he rescued an old man from a Buick that had slid off into a storm-swollen river. Then he turned right around and swam back to rescue his dog."

"What was his name?"

"Whose?"

"The dog."

"Rover." Rick grinned. "Heck, how should I know? Are you trying to get back on my good side?"

"I didn't know you had a good side." He winked and she felt her face flushing as he ate the last of his bagel. "I had to ask that question. In spite of the fact that I believe you'd have told me up front if you suspected Adler had anything to do with Sylvia's murder. Particularly, knowing my past as you do."

"How are you dealing with that?"

"I don't want to talk about it." She stood up and tossed her trash into a nearby can. "Let's go back across the street and talk to Heidi Udall."

"The woman from The Rabbit Hole?"

"One and the same."

"She'll know we're coming."

"How do you know that?"

"ESP." He winked again and she socked him in the arm. "Don't look now, but I believe that's her peering out the window of Batter Up."

Julia glanced in the direction of Heidi's display window. There was the baker and owner, all right, the nosiest woman in town trying to hide behind her curtains. She appeared to be watching them across the street.

But Heidi might be looking at Laney and the chief of police, leaving her shop and climbing into Laney's SUV.

Laney took off at a moderate speed then suddenly she was burning rubber. Had they found out something relevant to their case or was she just letting off steam?

Dana often teased her that she was in the wrong profession.

Ana would usually add, deadpan, that she knew where Laney could get a good racecar. Cheap.

"Where'd you go, Julia?"

"Nowhere." She'd always been a multi-tasker, going in twenty different directions at once. But she'd never been one to lose sight of the immediate goal. Julia made herself focus. "You take the lead with Heidi."

"Why? You know her."

"Yes, but she doesn't think I'm cute."

Rick snorted and they headed off to Batter Up.

~

The interior of Heidi's bakery was a mess. Powdered sugar and stray napkins on the floor, half-carved pumpkins scattered about in no particular order, orange and black streamers loose and flapping from the ceiling. When Julia first moved to Shutter Lake, Batter Up was so clean you could eat off the floor. Though the tidiness had declined lately, Julia had never seen it this unkempt.

"Good morning, Heidi."

Heidi returned Julia's cheerful greeting with a mumble that sounded like good morning but could just as easily have been bug off. She'd probably been watching out the window when they went into The Grind. Her rivalry with Nolan Ikard was well known around town. Heidi considered his bagels a deliberate ploy to ruin her morning doughnut sales.

"You remember my friend Rick from last night at The Rabbit Hole."

The portly baker made a lightning transition from surly to flirty. "Of course!" She held out a plump hand dripping with flour. "Welcome to my sweet shop. Everything here is fresh. Made this morning by my own little hands."

Though Heidi was short, there was nothing small about her hands. They were large and broad with long fingers. Strong hands that could knead dough for the long hours required to run a bakery.

Or kill a person.

Julia willed herself to stop thinking like a reporter covering crime.

Rick was standing beside her still holding onto Heidi's hand, totally ill at ease. It was almost comical, a man too handsome for his own good, speechless over a woman's fawning.

Julia tugged his sleeve. "Rick, why don't we get some of Heidi's doughnuts? They look absolutely delicious."

Rick flashed a look of gratitude more appropriate for being rescued from the Titanic than from a slightly disheveled baker with flour on her hands and something else entirely on her mind.

Lust for Rick? Animosity toward Julia? A combination of those things, or something else entirely?

"What do you recommend, Heidi?"

"Cinnamon sprinkle doughnuts with butter cream filling, definitely."

"Great. We'll take half a dozen of those and I'll just step out of the way. Rick wants to talk to you."

Heidi fluffed out the hair – gray with white streaks - spilling from her baker's hat. It looked as if she'd just crammed the hat on her head this morning without bothering with a comb or brush. She was usually far more careful with her grooming. What in the world was going on?

She studied Heidi more closely. Her eyes were reddened and slightly watery, a look Julia had seen in the alleys and on the back streets of Chicago.

Her nerves tingled as she took the bag Heidi offered over the counter.

"Thanks." Julia didn't have to send Rick a signal. His entire body went on alert as she stepped aside and he closed in on Heidi.

Julia chose a table close to the display case where she would have a good view of Heidi's face. You could tell a lot about a person by looking into their eyes when they talked, and she didn't intend to miss a trick.

Rick smiled at the baker. "I hope you don't mind letting us take up a few minutes of your time."

"Of *course* not." Heidi's attempt at a twinkle was ruined by the alarming state of her eyes. "Ask anything you want. I've got all the time in the world for you."

She'd just told the truth. Julia leaned back in her chair and wondered briefly if she should eat a doughnut to keep Heidi in a good mood or if buying half a dozen of the wretched things would suffice.

Granted, they were delicious. But, oh, all those calories. And that bloated feeling when you woke up in the morning and regretted your previous day's sugar intake. Still, she decided eating one might help their cause.

"Heidi…is it all right if I use your first name?"

"Well, *naturally*. We're all friends here, Rick."

Julia didn't know whether she was going to gag on Heidi's response or on her doughnut.

"I'm in Shutter Lake to find a good friend, and I really need your help."

"I'm always willing to lend a helping hand. I'm big-hearted like that. Ask anybody in town."

A lie. If Heidi was big-hearted, Julia was a giraffe. Most folks in Shutter Lake loved Heidi's sweet treats but merely tolerated her. Dana was the exception. Generous-hearted Dana who always wanted to see the good side of everybody.

"I'm also looking for Josie Rodriguez. Have you seen her lately?"

Alarm skittered across Heidi's face. "She works part-time at Sparkle and used to come in here all the time. But now that I think about it, I haven't seen her in a while."

"How long since she was here?"

"I don't remember. Usually, I could tell you to the exact day when Josie was here. My mind's a steel trap, you know. But lately I've been so busy with personal matters I haven't kept up with my customers."

Heidi was telling the truth. Julia would swear on it.

"The last time you saw her, was she with anyone?"

"No. That much I remember."

"Did you have any conversation with her?"

"No, she's a quiet one. Never talks much to anybody that I know of except the Windermeres and Sylvia. God rest her soul."

Big lie. Julia read Heidi's body language, and it certainly didn't convey well wishes for Sylvia's soul.

"One more thing," Rick said. "If you don't mind taking a look at this photograph."

He handed her the picture and Heidi's face closed up like a moonflower at the first hint of sun.

"I've never seen him."

"His name is Evan Adler."

Heidi's gaze darted to Julia then over to the corner where a life-sized stuffed witch was about to lose her hat. It sat at a rakish angle on her stringy hair, and one of her black boots had come loose and was lying under a nearby table.

"Never saw him. Never heard of him."

Another lie. Another frantic survey of the room, as if Heidi were looking for a way to escape.

"I was really hoping you had some information that would help me."

Rick's pause was meant to solicit information, but Heidi just pursed her lips. Not a good look for her.

"He was here about a week ago," he added, "if that helps you any."

"I'm sorry. I stay so busy here creating a little bite of heaven for Shutter Lake, I really don't have time to notice who comes and goes."

Big lie. Heidi could be called the town crier. She made it her business to know everything about everybody in town. And whatever happened to that steel-trap mind she was bragging about? Today the baker was just full of contradictions.

"You didn't hear anything about my friend while he was here?"

"No. Like I said, I'm really, really busy." Heidi studied her surroundings as if the pots and pans might jump off the shelves and into her busy hands.

"I'm surprised, Heidi. And disappointed." Rick paused to let that sink in, but Heidi's face and body language telegraphed her refusal to cooperate. Whatever she wanted to hide was much more important than the fleeting chance she might catch the eye of a handsome stranger.

When Heidi didn't respond, Julia thought Rick would give up. He surprised her by saying, "My friend was spotted at both The Rabbit Hole and The Grind. I guess you just weren't looking out your window that day."

Heidi looked as if she wanted to smash a pan of hot butter cream into his face.

"I guess not. That's all I've got to say today. Unlike some folks, I'm going to the Bible study at Shutter Lake Church."

Heidi shot a venomous look at Julia then marched off in a huff toward her kitchen in the back of the shop.

Julia found enough self-control to wait until she was on the street before she dumped the sack of doughnuts into the garbage can. Like everything else in Shutter Lake, it was designed to make the town look as if it nobody would think of producing garbage. The can was hidden inside tasteful wooden slats, and the lid was attached by a chain so it wouldn't fly off and allow refuse to blow all over the cobblestone streets.

"That went well," she told Rick.

"You said Heidi thought I was cute."

"No. What I said was, she doesn't think I'm cute."

"Same thing."

"Are you going to be grouchy just because you couldn't charm Heidi Udall's pants off?"

"Looks that way." They climbed into his Explorer and he slumped against the leather seat. "She lied to me about everything."

"Yes. Almost everything."

"I think you're right about the connections, Julia."

"I'm always right."

"Smart mouth." He drummed his fingers on the steering wheel. "When Adler said he was coming here on personal business, I assumed he was coming to see a girlfriend, or maybe relatives."

"Does he have a girl fiend? Family?"

"I didn't know about his love life. We're both private in that regard. But I know his parents, even visited once."

Was Rick softening with age? Five years ago he'd been hyper-focused on his job to exclusion of everything and everyone else. Except Julia.

"Where are they from?"

"Nevada. Nice couple. Evan's dad is an engineer, his mom's a school teacher. They called me, desperate, when they didn't hear from him."

Rick looked so disheartened he roused Julia's mother-hen instincts. Thankfully that was all he roused.

"Maybe you ought to give his parents a call and ask if he has a girlfriend. If he did and she lives here, that would be a good indication I'm putting the facts together and coming up with the wrong answer."

"Not yet. They know I'm out here looking, and if I call they'll want to know what I've found out. I can't lie to them. And I can't bear to hear them hurting when they find out I haven't discovered a single clue that would lead me to his whereabouts. Besides, if they were aware of anyone here that he knew, they would have told me to check with that person first. I'm at my wit's end here."

"Don't be hard on yourself, Rick. We're just getting started. Are you hungry?"

Back in Chicago, Rick had always been hungry. If he didn't have such a finely tuned metabolism, he'd probably weigh three hundred pounds.

"I was, but you threw away all the doughnuts."

"You want to grab a bite of lunch?"

"No. Let's press on. Where to next?"

"The Windermeres."

"Of the Windermere Center for the Arts?"

"The same."

"Even the name sounds intimidating."

"You're going to love them, Rick."

"As long as they don't think I'm cute."

Chapter Five

They are after me.

Heidi stood at her window, hidden behind a curtain so she could watch that skinny bitch Julia Ford turn tail and run. She climbed into a Ford Explorer with Patrick Richardson and they drove off. Good riddance.

First, the cops were nosing about her shop asking about Nolan Ikard. He'd opened up The Grind this morning then raced off like a scared rabbit. Going straight to hell, she hoped. He'd been trying to ruin her business for years. Oh, yeah, she'd seen him all right, but she wouldn't mention it to the cops if you deprived her of sugar for a month. She wasn't about to give herself away by acting like she knew a single thing related to Sylvia Cole's murder.

As if that weren't enough to turn Heidi gray, that swizzle stick Julia Ford had marched in acting all high and mighty, like somebody famous instead of a has-been working down at that silly weekly rag.

She'd shut up fast when Heidi mentioned Shutter Lake Church. Julia didn't have a clue the Bible study was not 'til afternoon. When she bothered to darken the church doors she sat in the back like she had something to hide. Good people sat on the front pew, like Heidi.

Who cared that Julia Ford also had a lifestyle column in that daily over in Sacramento? The *Sacramento Bee,* she thought it was called. Heidi didn't waste money subscribing. She didn't care what Julia had to say about the Windermere's attire at the symphony and what they served at their so-called fancy fundraisers.

Heidi already knew. She went to every one of them. Never missed a bite. They called that silly bird meat covered up with unappetizing sauce *gourmet* food.

She could cook their caterers under the table any time of day. If they wanted real food, why didn't they call her?

She was more than a baker. She'd studied the culinary arts. Briefly. She knew how to truss a turkey and flambé peaches. But did those high and mighty Windermeres give her a chance to showcase what she could do? Oh, no! They had to go all the way to

Sacramento to get their caterer. Sometimes they even hauled in one all the way from San Francisco.

At least the Windermeres always sent her an invitation to attend their events.

The stuck-up Coles, Yolanda and Zion, never invited her to one of their stupid patio parties. Not that Heidi would have gone. She loathed that greedy bitch Sylvia Cole. She was glad she was dead. Glad, glad, *glad!*

If they ever got her in the ground, Heidi was going to make a special trip to the cemetery just to spit on her grave.

Sure, she saw Sylvia with that FBI guy, Adler. But after what Heidi had done she wasn't about to say anything to anybody. Let alone that nosy string bean, Julia Ford. Next thing she knew Julia would be writing a sensational feature about Heidi just to get a foot back in the door of real journalism.

Who did she think she was, coming in here in the middle of Heidi's busy morning, sitting over there mincing at a doughnut and laughing while Patrick Richardson pried into her business?

He'd acted more like a cop than a cute man with boyfriend potential.

Oh, God. What if he was?

Heidi's stomach churned. Was he one of those big city detectives working undercover? Had he been trying to remain incognito by asking stuff about a missing friend when he was really after Sylvia's killer?

Oh, even worse, what if he was FBI? What if he already knew what Heidi had done? Would she end up in a federal penitentiary?

She'd starve to death on prison food.

What if they were just trying to get a confession out of her? What if they came back and arrested her? She had to do something.

She glanced around her shop as if a frantic search might conjure up Sheena Appleton. Heidi hated using that skinny freak, never called her unless it was an emergency. People who looked like bean poles shouldn't be allowed near a sweet shop. It was bad for business. Still, you'd think Sheena might stop by occasionally just to see if her occasional boss needed some help. After all Heidi had done for her, showing her how to improve her dubious baking skills, you'd think she'd show more gratitude.

Finally giving up the illusion she could conjure Sheena out of thin air, Heidi locked her door and put out the CLOSED sign.

Then she flung aside her hat and apron. They landed on the stuffed witch in the corner, but she didn't care. She had to get out of there. Go somewhere.

But where?

Frantic, she searched her shop again for answers. That stupid witch leered at her from under Heidi's chef's hat. She marched over and kicked the stuffing out of her.

"Stupid, stupid, stupid!" With each kick, she wished the witch were Sylvia.

Another awful thought slammed her. Why was he asking about Josie? Where in the hell was she?

Sweat rolled down Heidi's face and dampened her hair. It stuck to her neck like seaweed. Heidi's last kick sent the witch flying toward the display case where it landed atop a freshly made German Chocolate cake.

Good. Heidi would just eat the cake herself. She nabbed it on her march toward her office in the back of Batter Up. With one hand she dug a finger into the icing and with the other she opened a desk drawer and scrambled around for a scrunchy to tie up her hair.

"Think. *Think!*"

Troy Duval. That's who she needed to see. Desperately.

Heidi fortified herself with another bite of icing then raced back to the front of her shop and stuffed six chocolate sprinkle doughnuts into a bag for Troy.

Make that a dozen. She was generous that way.

Never mind that Troy watched his sugar intake and today wasn't Wednesday.

Dana Perkins had paid her to take bagels to Troy every Wednesday. That had been the day Sylvia personally cleaned his house, and Saint Sylvia had always taken him a bagel. What a joke!

The only reason Heidi agreed was because Dr. P. was the only person in this rotten town who was genuinely nice to her. Nearly everybody else looked at her like she was a fat freak. If they bothered to look at all.

Heidi was an astute judge of character. Dr. P. had gone to the rescue of a chubby little girl in a pink dress — one of Heidi's customers in Batter Up — who was being bullied by a boy at least two inches taller. Dr. P. had set him straight without making a big fuss over it. She was so nice even the boy's mother had thanked her.

Heidi grabbed her purse and was racing toward her back door when she remembered Dr. P. had told her to call Troy first and let him know she was coming. He lived like a reclusive royal in his gated house.

She backtracked and made the call from her office so she could write on one of the pink scratch pads she kept in the top right hand drawer. Troy gave her a temporary code to punch into the keypad at his gate. Fancy. A little too fancy for Heidi's tastes.

She was about to head out again, but on second thought she grabbed an extra dozen doughnuts. After her visit to Troy – oh, and then the church group – she'd drop them off at Shutter Lake School where Dr. P. was principal. Maybe they'd sit down and have a coffee break together. Maybe Heidi would invite her over to help put the finishing touches on the Halloween decorations in the shop.

She probably wouldn't tell Dr. P. she'd taken doughnuts to Troy.

No. She *definitely* would not.

~

The winding driveway to Troy's house took Heidi through his vineyards.

"Over the top," she muttered.

If *she'd* wanted to remain incognito she'd have certainly found herself a less ostentatious house. Who did he think he was fooling? Certainly not her. She'd been in Shutter Lake far longer than Troy Duvall, and she made it a point to know everything about everybody in town. You didn't have to be a detective to unearth secrets. She was nobody's fool. She had her ways.

Troy Duvall – not his real name, by the way – had left Hollywood up to his neck in scandal. Murder. Sex. Probably drugs, too. She hadn't heard that specifically, but she certainly knew the right people to ask.

Heidi punched the bell on his front door, and the scandal-ridden man, himself, let her in. She was shocked at how frail he looked, his once-thick silver hair thinning and his expensive clothes hanging loosely on his tall, thin frame.

Word had it, he'd adored Sylvia.

That bitch.

"Good morning, Mr. Duval!"

His soft, "Hello," was polite enough, but the perusal he gave her suggested she might have been out on Brenda Lockhart's ranch tromping around in fancy horse manure from her fancy horses.

To make matters worse, the sun was beating down, the temperature was rising and Heidi's hair was dripping sweat. It slid off the end of her nose and landed with a plop on the front of her shirt. Too late, she remembered she'd forgotten to twist her hair back with a scrunchy.

Had she even found one in her desk? How could she remember, standing in front of this dip shit? He didn't have the courtesy to let her in his house.

She held out the bag of doughnuts. "I brought you something."

"Oh, yes. Do come in." He took the bag of doughnuts and led the way inside.

Well, *finally*.

He walked like a miserable snail into a den big enough to fit her car, a Honda Civic. A sensible car for a sensible woman. She'd bought it used a few months back. She would have paid cash, but lately she was strapped.

"Won't you sit down, Heidi?"

She sank onto the sofa opposite the fireplace and leaned back, grateful to get off her feet. She could do without the fire, though. It cast a glow over the wheelchair, which Troy ignored. Instead he sat in a large overstuffed chair adjacent to Heidi and pulled a lap robe over his legs.

"Won't you get hot under that?"

"No." He indicated the teapot and two cups on the table beside his chair. "Would you like some tea, Heidi? I made Vanilla Chai. It was Sylvia's favorite."

"No, thank you." Heidi wouldn't be caught dead having the same thing that greedy bottom-feeder liked. "I had a cup before I left the shop." It was a lie, but he wouldn't know the difference, especially when she got through telling him about *her* morning. "It's a lovely way to take a break after the morning rush. So soothing. Really. It's the only way I can relax after I've been up at the crack of dawn frying dough and baking the best cakes and cupcakes this side of heaven. Then half the population of Shutter Lake comes in

Batter Up asking for the one thing I didn't make that day. Can't they see in my display case? It's stupid! Sometimes I just want to pull my hair out. Or theirs."

She sucked in a deep breath. She'd gone so far off the rails with her tirade she had totally failed to find out if *she* was a suspect in Sylvia's murder. "But, oh my, there I go talking about my problems when I really wanted to ask you if the cops have any new suspects in Sylvia's murder. Like, anybody local? "

There, she'd said it. The smile she turned in his direction made her face feel like rigor mortis had set in.

"I'm not privy to the details of the investigation."

"But you adored Sylvia and knew her better than anybody else in this town. I was just sure Zion and Yolanda would keep you informed."

He shook his head, *no.* And why was he looking at her at like she'd suddenly grown horns?

"Well, maybe you can help me out with this. What was Sylvia doing hanging around with Evan Adler? He's FBI! And why was Julia Ford all up in my business this morning unless somebody thinks *I* had something to do with knocking Sylvia off? Why, I'm a pillar of the community and practically an icon at the church!"

"I'm sure you are, but Sylvia was a private person. I can't help you with any of that."

"You can't, or you won't?"

Troy studied her so intently it made her squirm. "What are you on, Heidi?"

"What do you mean?" He just stared at her. The old peckerwood. She patted her hair, alarmed to find it soaked. "Is that any way to treat a guest? Somebody who has taken time from her busy day to bring you a treat? Why, I closed my shop for you!"

"I appreciate the doughnuts. But the question still stands."

"So does my answer." She shifted her weight, looked at her feet and noticed with dismay that she was wearing one black shoe, one navy. She tried tucking one foot under the sofa, but her legs were too short. "I can't believe I drove all the way out here for you to quiz me like this."

"I'm trying to help you, Heidi."

"If you call this being helpful, I'd hate to be the brunt of your anger."

"I sometimes wonder if I could have prevented Sylvia's

murder. Such an amazing young woman. I can't sit idly by and watch the same thing happen to you."

Heidi nearly lost her German chocolate frosting. Didn't he know that woman was a trollop? Didn't he know she'd slept with Vernon Bradshaw right under his wife's nose? For Pete's sake, Sylvia had even reached out from the grave and nearly got the Bradshaw kid convicted for murder.

Still, what if Troy was right? After all, he used to be part of that Hollywood crowd. The same crowd that got her hooked.

She teared up then rubbed at her nose and sniffled. After what she'd done, there was more than one reason somebody might want Heidi dead.

"I don't mean to scare you. Maybe I can help."

"How?" Put on a Halloween mask and shout boo? Why, the man was practically wheel chair bound.

"I don't know yet. If you want to talk to me, I'll be glad to listen. And advise you, if I can."

"Maybe you know the man who got me started, Rafer Williams, an actor from LA. He said that 'other white powder' would make me lose weight and improve my social life."

Actually, he was a dog wrangler, tasked with walking the director's two basset hounds during filming. He wanted to be an actor, though. And probably would some day. He was that handsome.

"He's a two-bit thug. When was this?"

"Last year. In Grass Valley. I was asked to provide the craft services when that independent film company was over there filming 'Days of the Beast.' It was a huge honor and great advertising for Batter Up. Craft Services provides snacks to the entire cast and crew the whole time they're filming."

Oh, it had been so exciting! Being in the snack tent all day, hobnobbing with everybody from the lowliest gaffer to movie stars. All that attention. The feeling that she belonged, that she was appreciated.

"Is Rafer still supplying you?"

The answer was *yes,* but she didn't see how that was any of his business. In fact, she'd already told him too much. About the only thing she hadn't told him was that his precious Sylvia was blackmailing her.

"You won't try to interfere, will you? You won't tell anybody?"

"I'm no snitch, and I've no desire to get involved again in the Hollywood scene. I'm just trying to prevent another tragedy. I encourage you to drop by the clinic to see Dr. Ana Perez. She's excellent, knowledgeable and caring. She's helped me tremendously, and I believe she can help you get clean."

"I'll think about it."

"Do more than think, Heidi. If you don't stop using, you could be the next one found dead in Shutter Lake."

She couldn't get out of there fast enough. Troy Duval had a lot of nerve trying to tell her what to do when he didn't even have the guts to stick around Hollywood and clean up his own mess.

She started to snatch up her doughnuts and take them with her. But that would be hateful, and Heidi was not a hateful person. She believed in justice. That's all.

That's why she'd laid such careful plans to kill Sylvia Cole.

Chapter Six

As Julia directed Rick to the Windermeres' mansion, her tension matched his own. Thus far, the only sightings of Agent Evan Adler in Shutter Lake had been with Sylvia Cole. Since the parents had not mentioned her as a girlfriend or as someone he knew, they were flying blind.

And she'd learned nothing new about the Josie Rodriguez disappearance. That added significant weight to her visit with the Windermeres.

Up ahead, she could see the couples' sprawling house at the end of Olive Lane.

"Before we get there, I need to brief you," she told Rick.

"I thought you'd already told me everything."

"No, not everything. I was in the *Firefly* offices when Katherine Windermere came in to ask my boss about finding a hacker. To understand how unusual that is, you have to know that her husband is a high-tech wizard. He designed soft ware for deep-searching the dark web."

"So if she wanted to find anything on the web, even something hidden, she could go directly to him."

"Exactly. I suspect she feels her husband is hiding something from her or she is hiding something from him. Either way, this is not going to be an easy interview."

Sylvia Cole's murder case was a spider web spinning out of control, with threads branching in every direction. Julia knew Josie had worked for her, and now somehow Agent Adler was tied in with Sylvia.

And what did Josie's host family know about any of it?

Julia was uncomfortably aware that by continuing her maverick investigation, she was trampling onto territory that belonged to Chief McCabe and Laney. Because of their friendship, Laney would take a tolerant view, but Julia doubted McCabe would. He was old family Shutter Lake, a cop through and through. His dad had been Chief of Police before him. Though he was now in a nursing home with dementia, his reputation was still alive and well. Both McCabes were revered in Shutter Lake for their ability to keep the peace and discourage crime in an affable, laid-back way that enhanced Shutter Lake's image as the best-kept secret paradise in California.

"Penny for your thoughts." Rick glanced in her direction then turned his attention to parking in front of the Windermere's house.

"I'd feel guilty about nosing around if I didn't know all Shutter Lake's resources are going into finding Sylvia's killer before he strikes again."

"Well said. Put on that beautiful smile and let's get inside so I can watch you do your thing."

Julia decided to ignore the personal comment. She had much more important things on her mind than tamping down any ideas Rick might have about resurrecting a dead affair.

Tasteful fall harvest arrangements adorned the Windermere's doorway, but there were no decorations that could be labeled specifically for Halloween. No black cats, witches and goblins, just mums in varying shades of gold arranged with sheaves of wheat and pumpkins, not carved.

Julia was surprised when Katherine Windermere answered the door. Usually, it was Jimmy Sykes whose forbidding pock-marked face, broad shoulders and muscular build were enough to intimidate anybody who might intend harm to the Windermeres. Jimmy performed multiple functions for the couple, everything from butler, to chauffeur to bodyguard.

"Julia! How nice to see you."

Katherine extended both hands and smiled in a completely open and guileless way that said she had nothing to hide. Her gray hair fell casually about her shoulders, emphasizing her blue eyes. Her slacks, boating shoes and nautical styled blouse suggested she and her husband might be planning to sail on Shutter Lake or drive to the Pacific coast where their yacht was docked.

"Don't mind my clothes. Quentin's already at the boat dock on the lake and Jimmy's taking me to join him shortly. We thought a short sail this afternoon might help us clear our heads."

"That sounds like a great idea."

Julia made the introductions then Katherine led them into her formal living room. The centerpiece was a Steinway grand piano. Not the much smaller baby grand Julia had owned back in Chicago, but a concert grand appropriate for the woman who'd studied at Julliard and had once planned a career as a classical pianist.

The piano gave Julia the perfect segue into an interview about the arts in Shutter Lake.

"You don't mind if I tape you?"

"Not at all."

"It's remarkable that you and your husband have kept the Shutter Lake Symphony going for so many years."

"Since this town was incorporated, to be exact. Quentin had succeeded in business beyond his wildest imagination, and he was looking for a challenge, something that would benefit the community. Besides, we believe that the heart and soul of a town lies in the arts"

"The Windermere Center for the Arts and the many performances each year have certainly done that. You have a ballet season and a symphony season as well as the community concert season that brings in Broadway shows. Can you talk about the financial commitment it takes to sponsor all those programs?"

"We also have numerous art shows and literary readings at the center. But don't give us all the credit, Julia. We get an E.R. Carpenter grant, but keeping the arts going is really a community effort, one in which we take great pride. It takes more than you can imagine to pay for the various guest artists we invite from New York and Boston and Dallas. We also have our wonderful music director, Joseph Klein, on salary."

"He conducts the San Francisco Symphony Orchestra as well as the Shutter Lake Symphony Orchestra, doesn't he?"

"Yes. You've done your research, Julia. Additionally, we have to pay members of the Shutter Lake Symphony Orchestra."

"How many of them live in Shutter Lake and where do the others come from?"

"We have only ten in Shutter Lake who are members of the orchestra. Two of them teach violin and piano at Shutter Lake School, four teach private music lessons, the other four are retired musicians. The rest of the orchestra come from the music departments of Sacramento City College and California State University in Sacramento, as well as the William Jessup University in Rocklin."

"Tell me about the fundraiser for the arts tomorrow on the square."

Julia kept the tape recorder going while Katherine emphasized that there would be no admission fee. She and Quentin wanted every citizen in Shutter Lake to feel a sense of ownership in Windermere Center for the Arts, even if they came and enjoyed the food and music without a donating a dime.

The full orchestra wouldn't be there, but there would be plenty of strings and brass to do Beethoven and Tchaikovsky justice. The food would be catered out of San Francisco and would feature blue crab shipped in fresh from Maryland.

"This kind of event makes the community feel connected," Katherine added. "With Sylvia's unsolved murder hanging over us, we all need that."

"Yes, we do."

Julia sensed not one false note in anything Katherine had told her. At this point, she felt nothing but admiration for both Windermeres.

But she'd learned in her early days of investigative journalism that not all is as it seems. There was still the matter of the missing girl.

As she turned off her tape recorder and stowed it in her bag, Katherine invited Rick to attend tomorrow's fundraiser in the park. As if they would miss it. Everybody in town would be there.

Possibly even the person or persons who had murdered Sylvia Cole.

"I hope you don't mind just a few more questions."

"Oh, my dear, I thought we'd covered everything."

"This is not part of the interview. It's personal and off the record. Do you mind if I take a few more minutes of your time?"

There was a slight tightening in Katherine's expression and body language, one you'd hardly notice if you hadn't been expecting it.

"Of course not, my dear."

"Rick is looking for this man. Evan Adler." She studied Katherine as she showed her Adler's photo. Whatever shiver had passed through her earlier had now vanished. She was as composed as if she were sitting on the bench in front of her concert grand playing Chopin.

Katherine took her time with photo then passed it back to Julia. "No, I don't believe I have."

It was impossible for Julia to tell if she were lying. Katherine either had no knowledge of Adler or was a very good actress, which wouldn't be surprising. People gifted in one of the arts often possessed talent in the others.

"Are you sure? He seemed to be friends with Sylvia. And since Josie worked for her and lived with you, I thought perhaps you might have seen him."

Katherine's expression was still a study in innocence.

"No. I don't recall ever seeing him."

Julia hated what she was about to do. She genuinely liked Katherine Windermere, genuinely admired her civic spirit, her grace, her generosity. Still, skills she'd kept buried for five years were bubbling to the surface, and she reminded herself that two lives were at stake: Josie's and Adler's.

"I'd like you to think hard and be very certain."

Bingo! Katherine's expression suddenly became guarded. Her enormous wealth insulated her from many unpleasant things, including being pressured by the press.

"Evan Adler works for the FBI..." Katherine's face went a shade paler, a sign of vulnerability. Julia struck while her opponent was weak. "You came into the *Firefly* asking for the name of a hacker. Why is that?"

"It was nothing. Nothing at all."

"The request is most unusual, especially coming from a woman whose husband is a genius in that field. I was there at the newspaper that day. Remember?"

Katherine sat very still, visibly composing herself. Smart. She knew she'd made herself a target and she was shoring up her defenses. But what was she trying to hide?

Julia glanced at Rick, who gave her an imperceptible nod. His sign of approval.

She turned her attention back to Katherine. Now that Julia had rattled her opponent and shown that knowledge was her strength, she was ready to give the older woman a way to save face.

Softening her tone, she asked, "Did you remember anything you'd like to tell me?"

"I did. I changed my mind about the hacker. Truly. It was a ridiculous idea in the first place. But that's what happens when you age. You suddenly start getting ridiculous ideas."

Katherine Windermere showed very few signs of aging. Except for her silver hair and a sprinkling of laugh lines around her eyes when she smiled, she looked like a woman of forty-five instead of the sixty-something Julia knew her to be. Her skin was smooth and taut, and not due to cosmetic surgery. Katherine had none of the unnatural stretching around her mouth and eyes that would indicate she'd been under a plastic surgeon's knife. Like Julia's own mother, she was aging gracefully, and still a beautiful woman.

Julia made a humming sound that would pass for agreement. "Anything else?"

"About that young man. Adler, you said?"

"Yes."

"And he was FBI?"

"Yes, but we don't know why he was in Shutter Lake. We were really hoping you might shed some light on that."

"Now that I think about it, he came here once looking for Josie." Julia felt a shiver of excitement. Hope can hang on such a small thread. "Such a polite young man. Clean cut. Well-spoken."

"When was that?" Rick jumped in. "Do you remember?"

His sharp and pointed questions sent shivers through Julia. Each step of their investigation took them deeper into a quagmire that just might pull the whole town under.

"I don't remember dates unless I write them on my day planner. But, let me see…I think it was a day or two before poor Sylvia Cole was murdered. Of course, Josie wasn't here."

"Did Adler say why he was looking for her?"

"Oh, dear." Katherine was visibly rattled by Rick's questions. "I want to help you. I really do, but it was such a brief conversation I don't recall the specifics. I was on the way to a meeting of the symphony board and he never came inside."

Rick's slight nod indicated he wanted Julia to take over. *Good.* The whole point of the visit was to find out what Katherine knew, not crack her like a walnut. Suddenly Julia was reminded of her own mother, so like Katherine, elegant, charming, a supporter of the arts and a pillar of the community – an older woman who gave the impression that remaining relevant was easy. Not an easy task. Julia could only hope to grow old as gracefully as those two women.

"You're doing fine. Just fine." Julia smiled and some of the tension left Katherine's face. "Had you ever heard Josie mention Adler?"

"No. Not that I recall."

"You never heard her have a phone conversation that might have indicated she was talking to him? Or someone you didn't know?"

"I'm sorry. I didn't."

"When did you last see Josie?"

Katherine looked as if somebody had socked her in the stomach. Still, she was smart enough to take some time to get herself back under control before answering.

Finally she said, "I went with Quentin to put her on the plane to Venezuela."

"Which flight was that?"

Katherine couldn't remember the flight number, she didn't have any reason to, but she did remember the date and time.

"Are you sure she got on that plane?"

"Positive. We waited until she got through security. She turned around and waved to us. Such a beautiful child."

Katherine Windermere's poise was legendary, but in the face of Julia's questions about Josie it seemed over the top. Did the woman not know the exchange student was missing? Or was she somehow involved and covering it up?

Julia thought back to what Dana had said at girls' night out. She'd just begun to suspect something was terribly wrong about Josie's absence. With the entire town concentrating on Sylvia's murder, a missing exchange student could go unnoticed for a while. Now that Rick and Julia were asking questions about her, Josie's disappearance would soon become public knowledge.

"Why would a bright girl like Josie give up her opportunity to study at Shutter Lake and go flying off to Venezuela?"

The question shattered Katherine's famous poise and left her visibly shaken.

"A family emergency." Her response was tentative, uncertain and she looked close to tears.

"Still, why would a straight-A student who'd worked so hard to get one of the coveted slots as an exchange student give it up? Weren't there other relatives down there who could have helped in this family emergency?"

"I don't know how many of her family are left down there." Katherine's hand shook as she ran them through her hair. "Josie is very loyal to the people she loved."

"Mrs. Windermere, it doesn't make sense to me." Rick leaned toward her in the earnest way that made people want to respond truthfully to him. "What could a teenager do to help in the midst of a family emergency? Especially with a travel advisory out and the county in utter chaos."

"Oh, you're right. I *know*." Katherine took a deep breath, obviously fighting for composure. "I didn't question her decision. It didn't seem fair, somehow. I wanted her to stay so she could have a better future. But at the same time I didn't want to unduly influence her."

Katherine's face went wistful, and she seemed to be looking backward and inward. "Perhaps I made a mistake with Josie. Quentin and I never had children of our own, you know, though we could have given them every advantage. Perhaps we're lacking in some other way, some common sense way that allows mothers and fathers to instinctively know what's best for their children."

Katherine's voice cracked and tears coursed down her cheeks.

"I'm sorry." Julia squeezed Katherine's hand. "I know this is hard for you."

"Oh, I do hope she comes back soon. She's smart enough to make up for lost time at school. And next time she wants to leave school, I won't be such a foolish pushover."

Julie's assessment of Katherine took another sharp turn. If Shutter Lake's icon of the art world was up to her neck in intrigue, it had to be accidental. There was no way the woman sitting in front of her would deliberately set out to harm Josie or any other child.

She reached for Katherine's hand again. "Thank you for taking so much time to help us. I hope we haven't ruined your afternoon sail."

"Oh, my dear. I don't care whether I get on that boat or not. It was all Quentin's idea, the old darling. He'd stay on the water if I'd stay on it with him."

"You've been very generous with your time. Both Rick and I appreciate it."

"I'm always glad to talk arts with another musician. You do play piano, don't you?"

"I do. It was one of the many social graces my Southern mother thought I should learn."

"Good for her. We'll invite her to Shutter Lake when you're our guest artist at one of the symphonies."

"I play, but I'm not that good."

"I hear otherwise." Katherine Windermere's smile was genuine as she stood and linked arms with Julia. "And I can be very persistent."

"I've no doubt." She and the older woman went arm in arm to the door and Rick followed along behind. Funny, she hadn't noticed when she'd come in, but there was the scent of something good and clean in the Windermere house, lemon with a slight hint of jasmine, but also kindness and sympathy. Maybe even love.

Julia said a last goodbye and hurried outside before she turned into a wimp, a marshmallow, a silly sentimental fool.

The sun was past its zenith and riding high in a brilliant October sky. Her stomach told her it was way past time for lunch.

She glanced back over her shoulder. Rick was still standing with Katherine Windermere under her porch, the shadows turning him dark and dangerous.

He'd looked dangerous that day, too, the day she'd faced a thousand questions about her escape from the Jack o' Lantern serial killer. His outrage and personal feelings barely contained, Rick stood in a circle of law enforcement - FBI and half the Chicago Police Department - all waiting to talk to her about a madman who had left a trail of carnage across state lines.

Until Julia stopped him.

Until she killed him.

"Julia?" She jumped at the sound of her name, and Rick put a hand on her arm. "Where did you go?"

"You don't want to know. Don't ask."

"All right."

He escorted her around the side of the Explorer and opened her door, ever the gentleman. She didn't know why she let him. Her mother's training, no doubt. Or perhaps because the elegant Katherine Windermere was still in her doorway, watching.

Julia slid into the seat, chastising herself. She had to quit blaming every one of her shortcomings on her mother. Rachel was a good woman, an excellent mother, a wonderful wife and an asset to Chicago society. Julia could only hope to be half that successful as a human being when she got old.

Her mother would die to hear Julia thinking of her as *old*. Make that *as she aged*

"So, what do you think?" Rick shot her a look she remembered so well, that deep, assessing perusal that seemed to tap into her emotions.

"About what?"

"The beautiful and charming Mrs. Windermere. Was she telling the truth?"

"About Adler, I'd say yes. I think she doesn't know any more about him than she told us."

"Still, if he was looking for Josie, and if your friend Dana was correct, he might have been nosing around in trafficking."

"Which means, we should tell Chief McCabe and Laney what we've found out."

"Laney?"

"Holt. My friend, the deputy chief."

"Sounds like you've made friends in high places."

"There's more to Shutter Lake than meets the eye, Rick. And I'm not talking about the scenery. Or the murder, either. The people here are smart and basically good."

"Then you've decided to stay?"

"I don't know. My mother asks me that all the time. I came here to hide, but I might just end up staying."

"And where does that leave me?"

"With your wife."

Now Rick was the one who didn't want to talk. His grip tightened on the wheel and he stared straight ahead as he drove back toward the center of town. That infernal mask he wore had dropped into place. Julia couldn't have read him if she'd had access to an encyclopedia of the human mind with the magician Merlin thrown in for good measure.

Finally, he said, "About that talk with Shutter Lake PD."

"What about it?"

"I'm not here in any official capacity. I'm unofficially looking into the disappearance of a friend."

"Noted. And?"

"And, what?"

"I hear an *and* in your voice."

"You know me too well, Julia."

"I don't want to go there."

"All right. I'll concede. For now." He took the turn onto Main Street. "And… we don't have anything concrete to take to your Chief McCabe and Deputy Holt."

"When we do, we'll report it."

"Right… Hungry?"

"I am."

"Where to?"

"My house. I've had enough of people for a while. I need to detox."

Julia hadn't felt that way about crowds until she'd been taken by the Jack o' Lantern killer. Until she'd done the unthinkable. Then she'd found herself coming out of the dark shadows of captivity and facing a battery of reporters and cameras and cops - and an entire nation hungry for the lurid details. Suddenly she'd felt smothered. That had been the beginning of her panic attacks.

"Julia?" Rick touched her shoulder - softly, briefly – drawing her back from the darkness. "Do you still make that mean chicken piccata?"

Her gratitude was so enormous, so intense she felt like weeping on his shoulder. Since the Jack o' Lantern madman, she'd found it embarrassingly easy to be undone by the smallest, unexpected kindness.

"I do, but today you're getting a ham and cheese sandwich. Potato chips, too, if you're lucky."

"Works for me."

He made the turn at the corner of Main and drove the few blocks to Harmony Street. It was a relief to see her cottage come into view. Her home. Her haven.

Rick parked at the curb and killed the engine. "Let's go inside. I'm starving."

"You always are."

Julia let herself out of the passenger side and strode into the welcome peace of her home.

Today she didn't even mind that Rick was there with her. In fact, with a killer still on the loose in Shutter Lake, she realized she felt safer in the company of her long-ago protector.

Chapter Seven

While Julia made sandwiches, Rick worked on his laptop at the bar separating her kitchen from an Eastlake oak table, china cabinet and sideboard she'd found at Good Stuff in Grass Valley. She loved Eastlake's clean smooth lines, the low-relief carvings and simple geometric ornamentation. It was not fussy and heavy like the Victorian dining room set of her childhood. That had been a pain in the neck to dust. She'd been glad when mother finally ditched it for the minimalist look.

Julia glanced at the clock on her kitchen wall - black Art Deco, Great Gatsby style, another of her favorite eras. It was after two. No wonder Rick had said he was starving.

She opened a can of tomato soup with basil, added a chunk of cream cheese and zapped the whole thing in the microwave. Voila'. Instant tomato bisque. It was one of the gourmet food short cuts she'd shared with readers in her lifestyle column.

Rick looked up from his work. "Something smells good."

"Soup. I'm a regular Julia Child now. Any luck?"

He was working on his mobile phone as well as his laptop, using his contacts to find out if Josie had actually been on her flight to Venezuela.

"Not yet."

"Then let's eat. Maybe you'll find something after lunch."

"Let me wash up first."

"The guest bathroom is straight down the hall and to your left."

While he was gone Julia put the sandwiches on two china plates and divided the hot soup between two matching china bowls, Chateau-France design. Five years ago she'd found the American Limoges twelve-place setting at an antique store in San Francisco. Immediately, she'd known it was meant to be hers.

Never again would she eat from a plastic plate shoved under the door. Sometimes the monster had used paper plates. She no longer ate from those, either, unless she was at someone else's house or a public event surrounded by a crowd of people, most of whom she knew.

What was keeping Rick?

She added linen placemats and napkins, filled two crystal glasses with sun-steeped tea she kept in her refrigerator – everyday touches of elegance and beauty she'd adopted after her escape from captivity, promises to herself that she'd never be that vulnerable again.

Suddenly her cell phone played "Crazy." Julia dug it out of her pocket, moved to a patch of sunlight coming through the stained glass window above her sink and kicked off her shoes.

"Mom? What's up?"

"Since you're so stubborn about coming home, Joe and I are coming to see you."

Julia could picture it, Rachel descending on Shutter Lake like royalty in the midst of the town's only crime spree.

"When?"

"Well, I don't know that yet. Symphony season is in full swing and you know how the Chicago Symphony League depends on me. Maybe Joe can fly out there first. He wants to brush you up on your karate skills." Julia pictured her mother, twisting her pearls around her fingers as the talked, her mind racing with plans for her daughter. "Are you still practicing? Joe wants to know."

One entire bedroom of Julia's house was outfitted with her punching bag, a gym quality floor mat and every exercise machine she needed to keep her body and her skills sharp. Julia had learned from the best, her stepfather Grand Master Joe Chin. He had flown to Okinawa to study under the disciples of Gichin Funakoshi, founder of Shotokan Karate.

"Tell Joe I practice every morning."

"I will. He'll be pleased."

"Except this morning. Rick is here."

"Fabulous! He'll keep you safe."

Where had Rick been when she was being held in a dark basement? Where had the entire Chicago PD been when Julia went to a sleazy nightclub with the promise of a tip for the series of stories she was doing on the Jack o' Lantern killer? When she'd been knocked out with the date rape drug, hauled off to be dismembered and turned into a Halloween freak show by that depraved monster?

Julia felt the precursors of a panic attack.

No. I will not do this.

She took deep breaths, willing herself to come back from the shadows and into the sunlight of her kitchen.

She was strong. She would *not* be brought down by a panic attack. She, alone, had overcome the demented butcher.

"Mom, I don't need Rick or anybody else to keep me safe. I killed that depraved criminal with my own bare hands."

Thanks to Joe. Thanks to the lethal movements of an ancient form of fighting.

"Don't talk about it, Julia. I can't bear to think of that dark time. All those days when I didn't know where my only child was, or even if she was alive or dead."

"I know you can't, Mom, and I'm sorry. But it's all okay now. You have to remember that."

Even as she soothed her mother, Julia wondered if it was time she talked about her past. Maybe if Dana and Laney and Ana turned the cleansing beacon of friendship into those dark, forbidden corners, the secrets would lose their power.

She stood in the patch of sunlight long after she'd ended the call, the phone still in her hand. Her mind struggled to come back from the past resurrected by her conversation with her mother.

And the awful murder of one of Shutter Lake's most beloved young entrepreneurs.

And the unexpected disappearances of Josie and FBI Agent Evan Adler.

Julia didn't know she was crying until suddenly she found herself wrapped in Rick's arms.

How in the world had that happened?

She was losing it.

"It's all right, Julia. I'm here. We'll work this out together."

"No." She pushed him away. "There is no *we*. I still have a few kinks to work out for myself. And you still have a wife."

She hadn't kept up. Hadn't wanted to. But her mother had. And Rachel was quick to inform her daughter of all things pertaining to the man she'd once considered her future son-in-law.

"We're getting a divorce."

"That's what you said the last time."

He had been so convincing, the very handsome agent with the easy smile and the stellar record. They'd met when she was doing an op-ed piece on law enforcement. Six months before she'd been taken by the Jack o' Lantern killer.

Rick had said he was separated. True. And getting a divorce. False.

To give him credit, maybe he'd believed it. It didn't matter now. Julia was moving forward, not backward.

"Let's eat before the soup gets cold." Julia stepped back into her shoes and led the way to her table.

Rick slid into the chair across the table from her. "You've changed everything in your bedroom."

"You were sneaking around my house?"

"The bedroom door was open. I observed. That's what I do."

"Then you couldn't help but notice last night that my living room is different, too."

"I noticed."

"Every stick of furniture in this house is new. Well, five years old, now. When I moved to Shutter Lake I got rid of everything from my old life."

"Including me."

She held her hand in a traffic cop *Stop* signal, and he had the grace to look chagrinned. "The only thing I kept from my other life was my baby grand. It's in my mother's living room."

"How's Rachel?"

"The same. She'll be pleased you asked about her."

"She's one cool lady. Tell her I said hello."

Why not? It would make Rachel feel good and it wouldn't change Julia's mind one iota. Rick was a closed chapter of her life.

"I will," she said and then concentrated on her food.

When Rick's phone buzzed, he glanced at the screen, mouthed *Josie* then disappeared into the kitchen to take the call. He gravitated to the same patch of sunlight she'd stood in only moments earlier.

She and Rick had always been alike in that way, seeking the light as a way to burn away the darkness that surrounded them in their work. Chasing criminals and reporting on the underbelly of crime had given them an instant bond. They understood each other's needs in ways that must have been very hard for his wife, a small-town preacher's daughter who had become a kindergarten teacher.

Don't go there, Julia.

She never spoke the woman's name. Wouldn't even let herself think it. Long ago, Julia had made peace with herself over Rick's wife. She felt nothing but compassion for the woman whose husband obviously didn't want to be in the marriage. She wished her nothing but the best.

And she certainly had no intention of letting herself become the prize at the end of Rick's rocky marital journey.

He came back to the table and slid into his chair. "Josie never got on that plane to Venezuela."

"Katherine saw her go through the security gate."

"Which could mean she met somebody beyond the gate and left of her own accord."

"Or she forgot something, went back to get it and missed the plane." Julia shoved aside her half-eaten sandwich. "There are half a dozen scenarios that explain why Josie not being on that plane was the simple mistake a teenager would make."

"And plenty more that raise red flags."

"Her connection with your friend Adler, for one. Why was he at Katherine's asking to see Josie?"

"And why was he spotted at The Rabbit Hole and The Grind with your dead girl?"

"There's one person in this town who knew Sylvia well enough to answer that question." Julia stacked the plates, silver and napkins and shot Rick a look that said *get a move on.* "Dishes don't march themselves into the dishwasher, Richardson. Grab the glasses, and make it snappy. We have places to go."

It was already mid-afternoon. If they were lucky they could make it in time.

Chapter Eight

Heidi didn't know if she'd make it in time.

By the time she got to Shutter Lake Church, the Bible study would already be in progress. She aimed her car in the direction of town, furious she had to navigate back down that pig trail that led through Troy Duval's vineyard. Stupid, stupid, stupid!

He'd kept her corralled with his nosey questions. She didn't care if he'd once been famous or that he'd lost his wife and daughter and his health, too.

Well, she cared. She was a good woman. But the state of his life didn't exempt him from common decency. That's what she'd meant. He had no right to grill her like that. She was the owner of one of the most popular stores in Shutter Lake and an outstanding, law-abiding citizen.

Well, maybe not that.

But she *was* Somebody with a capital S. In spite of what swizzle sticks like Laney Holt and Julia Ford thought.

They probably never ate more than two bites at a meal.

Which reminded Heidi she'd missed her lunch. All on account of doing a good deed for Troy Duval. The fact that he'd not returned the favor by telling her a single thing about that bitch Sylvia's murder investigation still stung.

The bag on the front seat had turned greasy sitting in the closed-up car in the sun while she visited with Troy. The smells wafting from it made her mouth water. All those lovely doughnuts.

Heidi reached in and took two. They would tide her over till after Bible study. And she'd still have ten to take to Dr. P.

She chewed a while in satisfaction. Well…they barely made a dent in her hunger. What would three more hurt? Her hand closed around the doughnuts. She might as well make that four, and she'd still have an even half-dozen to drop by the school. Plenty to start a friendly conversation over coffee. She hoped Dr. P. had plenty of sugar and real cream. Not that artificial sweetener and all those chemicals they called powdered creamer. That stuff would poison you.

Heidi swerved and nearly went off the road.

That bitch Julia Ford knew. Last night she'd sat right there by Heidi at the bar in The Rabbit Hole and announced she was wearing a perfume named Poison. And then all those nosy questions from her friend this morning, pretending he was looking for a man named Evan Adler. Heidi *knew* Julia Ford was sitting in that chair looking smug because she was on the hot seat and that skinny bitch was trying to pin murder on her.

Yes, Heidi had meant to poison Sylvia Cole. Yes, yes, yes! The greedy, blackmailing slut. What right did she have to extract money from Heidi to keep silent about that other little white powder when Sylvia was trying to steal another woman's husband?

Heidi had fixed her, all right.

She was having a little rodent problem in the alley behind her shop, she'd told the clerk at the farm supply store. He'd suggested rat traps.

She'd gone all the way to Grass Valley. Heidi was nobody's dummy. She'd gone there three times over the course of this past summer and fall just to establish how bad the rat problem was. In case anybody started nosing around after Sylvia croaked.

Heidi had even mentioned the rat problem to Nolan Ikard. She just thought he'd like to know, she told him. After all, they shared the alley. It wasn't like the rats were entirely hers.

Her plan had seemed so easy. Foolproof…

Nine days ago

Heidi locked the door at Batter Up at noon, hung out the Closed sign and turned off all the lights in the front of the shop. If anybody questioned her later, she'd say her weak bladder was bothering her. Who could argue with sickness? Besides, it was her shop. This wouldn't be the first time she'd closed early.

She went into her kitchen to assemble her ingredients for cupcakes. Sugar, flour, rat poison.

She hummed as she worked. All those lovely cupcakes! She'd deliver them to Sylvia when she made her blackmail payment this afternoon.

Her final payment.

Heidi put her lethal confection into the oven and turned on the vent. She didn't want to risk getting sick from the fumes.

While the cupcakes baked, she whipped up her most sought-after icings, butter cream, strawberry, chocolate delight, caramel cream. She tasted each one first then added that extra special ingredient. More rat poison.

She could imagine it. The convulsions. The bulging eyes. Foaming at the mouth. She wanted Sylvia to suffer just as she'd made Heidi suffer.

An eye for an eye.

Heidi finished her deadly offering then boxed the whole thing up in one of her beautiful Batter Up boxes. Then she removed her baker's hat, climbed into her car and drove to Olive Tree Lane.

Heidi never called first. Sylvia had been explicit about that. She had a strict schedule for regular payments, cash only. If Heidi missed one, Sylvia would assume a life-and-death situation had intervened. If she missed the second, Sylvia would make sure everybody in Shutter Lake knew Heidi's dirty little secret.

Her business would be ruined. Her reputation. Her life.

Sylvia met her at the door. The strumpet was smiling as if they were best friends and this was a social call.

Well, fine. Today it suited Heidi's purposes to play that game. She smiled back.

"I brought you something. A peace offering."

"How sweet of you, Heidi." Sylvia took the box and held the door open. "Do come in." She led the way through her pristine house to the kitchen.

The house was empty of other people, as usual. Sylvia was hugely popular in town and was renowned for the good deeds she did and the awards she received for Sparkle. But she made it known her private life was just that.

It was only because of Heidi's intelligence and street smarts that she knew about Sylvia's affair with Vernon Bradshaw.

"Sit down, Heidi. I'm glad to see you're finally taking all this so well. We're just two enterprising women trying our best to get through life. Right?"

Heidi wanted to claw her face off. "Right."

Sylvia set the box of cupcakes on the bar and lifted the cover. "Hmmm. They look delicious. Let's have coffee and cupcakes to celebrate this turning point in our relationship."

Excitement made Heidi tingle all over. She hoped it didn't show. Her plan was going exactly as expected. Sylvia Cole would die right in front of her eyes.

"Great. But just coffee for me. I'm on a diet."

"Oh, that's too bad." Sylvia poured two cups then set a silver tray with cream, sugar and a sterling silver spoon on the bar in front of Heidi before settling onto a bar stool. "I am too."

The bitch! Heidi should have known. But what could she do? Put rat poison in Sylvia's granola?

Telling herself to play it cool, Heidi added two spoons of sugar and a generous helping of cream to her coffee then took a fortifying sip.

"The great thing about cupcakes is that they'll keep in the refrigerator for days! And then if you get the feeling you can't go one more minute without sugar, you've got a butter cream cupcake waiting for you. Or do you prefer strawberry? I made both. Chocolate and caramel, too."

Was she overdoing it? Sylvia was no dummy. She was eyeing Heidi over the rim of her coffee cup. Was she suspicious?

Heidi downed some more coffee and another awful thought occurred to her. What if Sylvia didn't eat a single one of the cupcakes? What if she carried them to Sparkle and the whole damned staff died of rat poisoning?

"On the other hand," Heidi said, "if the cupcakes are going to be a terrible temptation for you, I'll just take them back to Batter Up. Day-old cupcakes always do well for me. Reduced prices, and all that."

"Oh, no. I love all those icings." Sylvia closed the box and put it in the refrigerator, and there went Heidi's chance of redemption. "I hate to end our lovely chat, but I do have other business to attend to."

"So do I."

Heidi pulled the envelope of cash out of her purse and laid it on the bar. Sylvia had been explicit about that, too. She never took the payment directly in her hands. Heidi didn't know what the difference was between taking it directly and picking it up later, and she didn't give a shit. She just wanted to get out of there. The sooner the better.

"I'll see you same time next month, Heidi!"

"Oh…absolutely. Next time I'll bring a cake. I make a delicious sugar-free version of German chocolate."

"That sounds wonderful. 'Bye, Heidi."

Heidi's stomach was churning and her heart was racing so hard she thought she'd have a heart attack right in front of Sylvia's house. She made herself drive off at a sedate pace. The minute she was around the corner, she pulled over and vomited on the curb.

~

Recalling those poisoned cupcakes still sitting in Sylvia's refrigerator and her DNA on the curb a block from the dead girl's house, Heidi got so upset she reached into the bag on the seat of her car and ate the last six of Dr. P's doughnuts.

Fine. She was in no state for a casual visit to the school, anyhow. She'd do well to get through the Bible study.

As she'd predicted it was already underway in the gathering

hall at Shutter Lake Church. They stopped in the middle of the Beatitudes to exclaim over Heidi and ask if everything was all right.

"Of course." She took her usual seat in the center of the circle and explained she was late because she'd delivered a sweet treat from her own shop to Troy Duval, poor thing, almost a shut-in and so despondent over dear Sylvia's death. "Actually, I've been taking him a treat every Wednesday since her unfortunate death."

Heidi gave them a modest, self-deprecating smile and conveniently left out Dana's part in the plan as she explained that she, herself, had been so busy taking care of the needs of others she'd neglected her own appearance.

The church ladies complimented her on being such a great entrepreneur and fine Christian. They exclaimed how lucky they were to have her in the church.

Maybe they were sincere. Maybe they actually liked her. Maybe she'd give up that other white powder.

Heidi was too young to die.

Besides, she'd never even had any sex.

Chapter Nine

Rick climbed behind the wheel of his Explorer and Julia directed him to the medical clinic on the west edge of Shutter Lake.

"So, tell me about this Dr. Ana Perez," Rick said.

"She's beautiful, brilliant, compassionate. She could be working in any major medical center in the United States."

"So, how'd she end up here?"

"Nobody knows, really, but Shutter Lake is lucky to have her as a doctor and a part of this community. And I'm even luckier to have her as a friend."

"So you think as Sylvia's doctor she might have heard something that will be useful to us."

"She was also Sylvia's good friend. That's the connection I'm hoping will work to our advantage."

The medical clinic's parking lot was jammed with cars, not a good sign for Julia and Rick. Still, she counted on her friendship with Ana to get a few minutes of the doctor's time.

There were no carved pumpkins here, nothing to rot in the sun or become a breeding ground for bacteria. Instead, Ana's staff had plastered cutouts in the windows – black cats, witches, scarecrows and as a nod to the children, Charlie Brown sitting in the pumpkin patch awaiting the arrival of the Great Pumpkin.

As Julia and Rick approached the door, Nolan Ikard barreled through and bumped into her.

"Oh, Julia. Sorry."

"Nolan." He looked terrible - his face pale and drawn, his eyes haunted, his pullover hanging as if he'd lost weight. "We missed you at the coffee shop this morning. Are you sick?"

"Stomach virus. I can't seem to shake it."

"I'm sorry, Nolan. I hope you…"

He took off before the words *feel better* were out of Julia's mouth. He even took off without any sort of small talk, most unnatural behavior for the usually affable owner of The Grind.

"What's he running from?" Rick turned to stare after Ikard.

"Maybe Shonda called his cell and told him Griff and Laney were in the coffee shop looking for him this morning."

"That would be my guess. We need to talk to him as soon as he's over his stomach flu, or whatever the hell it is. He knows something."

"Maybe Ana does, too."

Rick pushed open the door to a packed lobby. "Looks like we'll be here a while."

"Not to worry. Come with me." Julia marched straight to the reception desk to ask her favor.

Less than ten minutes later, they were called to the back.

"Impressive." Rick put his hand in the small of her back. "You're the woman to know."

Before Julia could reply or shake off his hand, Ana came from one of the examining rooms, her long dark hair in a low pony tail and hanging down the back of her white lab coat, her dark eyes cataloging everything about Agent Patrick Richardson, including his hand on Julia's back.

She smiled as Julia made the introductions. "This way," she said and led them down the hall to her office. Vintage Ana. Direct, crisp and efficient. Her profession suited her perfectly.

"I'm sorry to take up your time, Ana."

"I can always spare a few minutes for you." That smile again. "But just a few. The clinic is packed to the rafters this afternoon."

"I saw. And we'll make it quick." Julia nodded and Rick showed the photo to Ana, identifying Adler as his partner in the FBI.

Ana showed no reaction to Adler's identity. Nor did she react when Rick told her Adler had gone missing in Shutter Lake about the time Sylvia Cole was killed.

"I don't recall ever seeing him."

"What about his car?" Rick described Adler's vehicle.

"I've seen plenty that might be mistaken for it in this town, but no, I can't say that I ever saw that car, specifically."

He nodded toward Julia and she took over. "Ana, Sylvia was spotted at least twice with the missing FBI agent, and Katherine Windermere said he'd also been at her house asking for Josie."

"And you think the three of them are tied together somehow?"

"Maybe. Did Sylvia ever mention Adler?"

"No. Not that I recall."

"Did she ever say anything that would lead you to believe

she'd been talking to him or an agent with the FBI?"

"She said nothing to lead me to that conclusion." Ana was perfectly composed, and yet there was an edge that told Julia she was either nervous or anxious to get back to her patients.

"Listen, Ana, thanks for making time for us."

"Not a problem."

"Just one more thing and we'll get out of your way. Did Sylvia ever mention Josie in any context other than a part-time employee at Sparkle? Maybe, that she wanted Josie to talk to Adler?"

"No. I'm sorry." Ana looked from Julia to Rick and shrugged her shoulders. "I really have to get back to my patients."

Rick thanked her and headed out the door, but Julia hung back.

"Ana, I'm sorry we barged in on you like this. I promise not to make it a habit."

"Not a problem. What's up with you and the hunk?"

"Rick?" Funny that Ana should refer to him as a hunk. Julia had stopped thinking of him in that way a long time ago. "Nothing. But I could use an emergency girls' night out."

"I could, too. But I'll be late."

"Aren't you always? See you at the Wine and Cheese House tonight. Sevenish."

Julia caught up with Rick outside the front door.

"So? Was your friend Ana telling the truth?"

"I don't know. Probably."

"You're usually very good at reading people."

"So are you, Rick. The problem with reading Ana is that she's smart enough to keep her real self and her real thoughts hidden from everybody, including me."

"Any other ideas? This is your town."

"It's getting too late to make business calls, and I don't think we ought to step on McCabe's toes by knocking on doors."

"It worked with Mrs. Windermere."

"Yes, but I can't trump up enough bogus interviews to justify it. Why don't we call it a day and I'll pick you up in the morning in time for the symphony on the park?"

"Works for me. I need to catch up on some of my case load."

Rick drove back to Julia's and parked on the street. The tension in the car was high, and not entirely due to the case of two missing people.

"I'll see you in the morning, Rick." She barreled out before Rachel's influence could take over her body and invite him in for coffee.

When she was inside, she pulled her cell phone out of her pocket to call Dana and Laney.

~

The Wine and Cheese House was at the opposite end of the block from The Grind. Julia probably wouldn't have spotted Griff McCabe's old Ford Bronco on a side street from The Grind if Laney hadn't told her that she and McCabe would be on stakeout.

Julia knew better than to ask Laney who they were staking out. She never talked about police business.

But it didn't take an investigative reporter to put two and two together. The cops had been in The Grind looking for Ikard this morning, Ikard had looked like death on wheels at Ana's clinic, and his hasty retreat tagged him as guilty. Of what, Julia didn't know. She'd never have pegged him for a guy who could commit murder. But then, she'd never seen the Jack o' Lantern killer coming, either.

Julia found a parking space and hurried into the restaurant, trying to ignore the row of glowing jack 'o lanterns that lit the pathway. Dana was already waiting at a booth in the back corner with a big platter of everybody's favorite stuffed mushrooms on the table in front of her.

Julia slid in beside her and ordered a chardonnay, thankful Dana didn't say a word until she'd leaned her head against the back of the booth and taken a deep breath.

"Better now?" Dana reached for a mushroom then shoved the platter closer to Julia.

"Some."

"Good. Eat. Take another breath. Talk can wait."

As Julia downed a mushroom she wished talk could wait until some magical time machine zapped them all back to Shutter Lake when it had been the perfect low-key, peaceful town. Before Sylvia Cole's murder changed everything.

She took a sip of her drink. "Laney's not coming. She's on stakeout down the street in front of The Grind waiting for Nolan Ikard."

"She told you this?"

"Good grief, Dana. Has the world come to an end?"

They both laughed at the idea of Laney telling them anything about the murder case. The release felt good, and Julia reveled in it a while before she filled Dana in on the things she knew about Laney's search for Ikard.

"They must have something or they wouldn't be staking him out." Dana nabbed another mushroom then leaned around Julia to see the front door.

"Ana said she'd be late."

"She always is. I just can't shake the feeling that I need to check on her. She hasn't seemed herself since Sylvia's death."

No one had. Not even Dana, who'd moved heaven and earth to prove that her student Vinn Bradshaw did not kill Sylvia. Julia figured that's why her friend was sugarcoating a brutal, cold-blooded killing by calling it merely *death*.

"You check on everybody, Dana. It's your mother hen nature. But I think you're right about Ana being a little off-kilter since Sylvia's murder.

"Ugh. Did you have to remind me a killer's on the loose?"

"Misery loves company?"

Dana swatted her with the dinner napkin. "You're not miserable, Julia Ford. You're one of the strongest women I know, and don't you ever doubt it."

"Yes, Mother Hen."

They reached toward the platter at the same time.

"We're going to have to order more mushrooms if we keep on eating like this."

"You're right." Julia grinned at Dana and both of them checked the door again for Ana. When she settled back with her drink she said, "You haven't asked about Josie."

"You'll tell me when you're ready."

"Sometimes I want to pinch you, Dana, just to see if you're real. You might just be the most controlled human being I've ever known."

"It comes from facing my demons. If you want to face yours, Julia, I've got your six."

"I know you have. You've guarded my secrets like Fort Knox." Everything from her past except her affair with Special Agent Patrick Richardson. She'd deliberately left that one in the dark. "I think I'm ready to talk about the Jack o' Lantern killer, but

I want all of you to be here. Including Laney. Sort of like a confession followed by an absolution from those who matter."

"Sounds reasonable to me. And healthy." Dana glanced at the door again. "Oh, here she is!"

She waved Ana over, and it took the three of them half an hour to catch up on the daily doings of each other's lives. It was the kind of soul-baring conversation Julia had missed in Chicago. Sure, she'd had her parents and a few co-workers she'd felt close enough to share a beer and a few meaningless details of her life.

With these wonderful female friends in Shutter Lake, she shared the details that mattered, the heart-wounds as well as the triumphs.

Julia glanced at Ana, who hadn't said a word about seeing her with Rick. And then she went straight to one of her old heart wounds.

"So...my friend from the FBI is in town helping me look for Josie."

That was her opening. Ana gave her a look of approval and Dana peppered her with a dozen questions about their search. Julia went over every bizarre connection between Josie, Sylvia and Adler, plus the dead-ends they'd discovered that could only point to a heart-breaking conclusion. The longer Josie Rodriguez was missing, the less likely they were to find her. Dead or alive.

"You've told Laney?" Dana asked.

"Not yet. It's too soon. Until Rick and I have something concrete, we don't want to distract the Shutter Lake PD from finding Sylvia's killer."

"That makes sense." Ana's voice was softer than usual. She seemed haunted this evening, possibly by the loss of her friend. Or possibly by Julia's and Rick's questions. Julia hoped she wasn't the cause of adding to her friend's burden. Heaven knew, Ana carried enough on her shoulders just taking care of the medical needs in Shutter Lake.

Julia reached over and squeezed her hand. "Tell Dana who you met this afternoon."

"Julia's friend, the incredible hunk."

"My ex-lover."

"Well, spit," Dana said. "You mean I asked you to bring a cast-off Romeo back into your life? A movie star look-alike at that?"

"Oh, yes, Evil One. You threw me to the wolf."

"If you tell me he ate you up, I'm going to lose my stuffed mushrooms." Dana's tart reply cracked them all up.

"He knows better than to bite off more than he can chew."

They were off and running again, laughing so hard tears rolled down their cheeks. And wasn't that one of the best things about having close friends? The freedom to be utterly silly and reveal deep truths at the same time, knowing your friends will never judge, never tell your secrets and never let you down. But best of all, knowing they will love you no matter how imperfect, reckless and sometimes just plain awful you are.

They ordered another platter of mushrooms, another round of drinks and then Julia told them of loving a man she'd believed was free to love her back. She told them of learning the painful truth – he had a wife who would never divorce him – and of the equally painful goodbye more than six months after they'd met.

"It was five years ago." Julia was surprised that telling her friends had been easier than she'd expected. "Right before I moved here."

"And he wants you back," Dana said.

"How did you know?"

"It's written all over your face."

"Well, Houdini. What's my answer?"

"A big fat NO."

"You've got that right."

Dana lifted her glass. "Let's all drink to that."

Chapter Ten

Griff desperately needed a drink. If he weren't staked out waiting for Ikard, he'd be home grabbing a cold beer from his refrigerator and watching football or an old John Wayne movie. Or he might be out at the barn saddling up Trigger for an evening run.

Hell, yeah, he'd named his favorite horse after Roy Rogers' famous mount. He loved the old cowboy movies, loved the idea that he was keeping the King of the Cowboys alive. Roy Rogers represented a simpler time when the good guys wore white hats and the bad wore black.

He wished it were that simple now. Since Sylvia's murder, everybody in his town seemed to be swapping hats at an alarming rate. Turns out, nobody was who they pretended to be.

Least of all, Griff.

His jaw tightened.

To make matters worse, there was the third member of that bunch Holt referred to as the girls' night out group. Ana Perez, walking into the Wine and Cheese House down the street. First Dana Perkins, who'd had her nose all up in his business after he'd arrested that kid Vinn Bradshaw for murder. And then that once-famous reporter, Julia Ford. Hell, she'd covered crime in Chicago. Won awards. Been cited on some of the best TV news networks in America.

It wouldn't take somebody with her credentials long to sniff out Griff's treachery.

Thank God the FBI was not with Ford.

But what was she doing a block away from his stakeout? Conducting a little stakeout of her own? Keeping tabs on him? Waiting for him to fumble this investigation so she could tell everybody in Shutter Lake that Griff McCabe was the last person on earth you'd want as Chief of Police.

For all he knew, Ford was already sharing the news with Perez and Perkins. The next thing he knew, she'd be telling Holt.

He glanced at his perfectly composed deputy. Under the street lights she looked like any ordinary beautiful woman. Until you saw her in action, you'd never guess how tough she was. Nor how compassionate. Laney Holt was the only person in Shutter Lake who knew the scope of his drinking problem, covered for him and still acted as if she respected him.

Anybody else in this town who happened to catch McCabe on those rare occasions when he couldn't hold his liquor assumed he was still hurting because his wife left him. Hell, he'd been over Janine so many years before she trotted out the door to enjoy big city life over in San Francisco, he'd helped her pack her bag.

Suddenly Holt turned to stare at him. "What's eating you, McCabe?"

"Nothing."

"That's a whole lot of fidgeting for nothing."

"I don't fidget."

"Well, whatever you call it, keep it down, will you? I'm trying to concentrate over here." Holt glanced up at Ikard's still-dark apartment over The Grind.

"What are you concentrating on? Ikard's nowhere in sight."

"If he's not back soon, I'm trying to think how I might break and enter his apartment without getting caught."

"Hell, Holt. You're sitting in the car with the law. I don't want to hear that shit." Her chuckle was low and wicked. "You keep that up and you're fired."

"You keep fidgeting and I quit."

Griff gave her the last word. He'd heard women liked that. Not that he cared.

Was it possible Holt herself had dug up his secret?

It had all seemed so simple back then...

~

Eight years ago

The day was still young when Griff rolled up to his house in his vintage Ford Mustang, powder blue, 1960s, a real honey of a car. His wife Janine had pitched a fit when he bought it last week, claiming he never paid enough attention to her, he spent all his time in the garage restoring old cars — case in point — his red 1950s Ford pickup.

What did she know? Nothing to do all day except paint her toenails and have lunch with her girlfriends at Stacked or Johnny's just down the block from the police station. He'd seen her parading in and out in her new outfits. If you wanted to talk about failings, how about her extravagant shopping sprees? And the way she colored her hair on a whim. He never knew whether he was coming home to a redhead or a brunette.

He was only a cop. It would take a Philadelphia lawyer to afford Janine and her expensive habits.

Still, he parked in the garage and went through the door that opened into the kitchen. It was five o'clock. Janine was right where she always was, sitting at the table applying red polish to her fingernails and carefully sipping a green concoction she'd tried to force on him.

"It's good for you, darling," she'd said. "All that fruit and spinach."

He'd take his spinach plain. His fruit, too. That's what he'd told her last week, and he'd tell her again. If there was one thing he could count on from his wife, it was her habit of bringing up a subject as many times as it took to get Griff to see things her way.

"Darling." She presented her cheek for his kiss. "The mayor called."

"What'd he want?" Griff shed his badge and gun. The mayor was a long-time friend of Griff's dad, Steve. Could this be about the alarming shifts in his dad's mental capacity?

"He didn't say. He's coming here at five thirty to talk to you."

There went his leisurely evening. He went through to their bedroom and shed his Shutter Lake PD uniform for a comfortable pair of faded jeans and an old tee shirt from his police academy days. He didn't care who was coming.

The only thing he disliked about his job was the uniform. It was stiff and constraining.

He passed back through the kitchen. Janine was right where he'd left her, her tongue caught between her teeth as she applied polish.

"When Mayor Crider comes, tell him I'm in the garage."

"Oh, shoot! You made me smear it."

The little-girl look on her face got Griff every time. He did love her. He wanted nothing more than to make his marriage work and start having children.

"It'll be okay, sweetheart." He cupped her face and kissed her on the lips. "Everything is all going to be okay."

She smiled and he went whistling off to the garage to pop the hood of his vintage pickup. By the time Mayor Carl Crider strolled through his kitchen door, Griff already had grease up to his elbows.

"My, boy! Your pretty wife said I'd find you here."

"Mayor Crider." He wiped his hand on his pants and shook the one Crider extended. "What can I do for you, sir?"

"It's not what you can do for me, son. It's what you can do for Shutter Lake." Crider outlined his plan to appoint a new Chief of Police. Griff's dad was retiring, not because of age but because of health. Crider extolled the virtues of having continuity, of giving the town a sense of security and stability by keeping a McCabe at the helm of law enforcement.

Griff admired his dad but he'd never aspired to head the SLPD. Too much responsibility. He was making it fine on a cop's salary. It was easy, low-stress work. The most taxing thing he'd done today was rescue the piano teacher's cat from a tree.

"The good thing about you as a candidate, my boy, is that you and the beautiful wife are a young couple who'll soon be having a bunch of little McCabes running around. People trust a family man. And they trust the McCabe name."

This promotion could be the answer to Griff's problem. A bigger salary and a higher social position would please Janine. And a happy wife would want children. The possibilities excited Griff.

"Yes," he said. *"I'll be glad to accept that position."*

"Well, now. Not so fast. I'm not the only one making this decision. There are others who think you might be too young. They're leaning toward Wilson Adams. He's a veteran on the force and a deacon over at the church, and his wife Barbara is a very popular kindergarten teacher."

They also had no children, and at their age weren't likely to.

"I thought you wanted a family man."

"There are some who will be pushing for maturity. Pushing strongly, I might add." The mayor pulled out a handkerchief and mopped sweat from his brow. *"I'm just asking if you'll let me put you up as a candidate."*

"I will."

"There are no guarantees. But I can tell you this, I will do everything in my power to see that you get the job. I owe it to Steve. He's a good cop, a good friend and a good man."

"Thank you, sir."

The mayor left by the garage door.

As Griff plunged back under the hood, he decided he wouldn't tell Janine until the promotion was a sure thing. No use getting her hopes up.

The kitchen door popped open and his wife raced over to hug him from behind.

"Darling, I'm so excited! I'll be the wife of the Chief of Police! I can't wait."

~

The truth – that Mayor Crider's offer was not firm – had set Janine on a five-day tirade of tears, screams and slammed doors. Particularly the bedroom door.

Still, Griff couldn't blame her for what he'd done.

He shifted positions in his seat then glanced over to see if Holt was going to nail him for fidgeting. Thank God, she didn't notice. Nor did she act like a woman who had ferreted out the real story behind Detective Wilson Adams' heart attack.

After two weeks of badgering and histrionics at home, Griff had planted drugs in his opponent's locker, easy to do when you're there every day and your dad is Chief of Police. Adams had been ordered into rehab, his name hastily withdrawn from consideration. He'd never be a cop again. He'd never even have a life again. His reputation in Shutter Lake was ruined, and his beloved wife of thirty years left him.

On the day Griff McCabe was sworn in as Chief of Police, Wilson Adams swallowed a full prescription of sleeping pills.

But nobody in Shutter Lake ever knew the real reason why.

The city's image had to be protected. Adam's widow had to be shielded. She was a beloved teacher. Destroying her as well as her husband would have spelled the end of the fairytale image of McCabe as law enforcement royalty and his city as an untainted jewel in the foothills of the Sierras.

Mayor Crider and Steve McCabe made sure the truth stayed buried. Now, with both of them in the nursing home – Griff's dad with Alzheimer's and the former mayor with a stroke that left his speech permanently garbled – no one would ever know.

Except Griff.

And all he could do to make up for destroying her husband was visit Barbara Adams at least twice a month to make sure she didn't climb on a ladder and hurt herself trying to change her light bulbs or put a battery in her ceiling-hung fire alarm.

She thought he was a saint. And that just might be one of the worst punishments of all for what McCabe had done.

"There he is."

Holt's exclamation jerked McCabe out of his dirty past and into the reality of Nolan Ikard creeping through the shadows in the alley between The Grind and Batter Up.

"Let's get him, Holt."

~

Questioning Ikard was the equivalent of repeatedly giving the gas to a car with a dead battery. Both of them were going nowhere.

Griff leaned against the wall with a cup of coffee and watched Holt in action. She'd already danced around Ikard's bellow, "How in the hell did you get my DNA?"

That old trope she'd told McCabe about guessing Ikard went on Geneology.Com and they got it didn't sit too well with the irate barista. But what the hell was he going to do about it?

He was in the police station being questioned by two cops who told him his DNA was all over the sheets and the bathroom of a murdered woman. A fact he'd loudly disclaimed. Twice.

"DNA does not lie, Ikard." Holt glared at the young barista who looked like hell. "Before you tell us again that you don't know how your DNA got all over the sheets in a beautiful woman's bedroom, you'd better think about that." She paused to let her latest shot sink in. "Sylvia was not just any woman. She's a murder victim."

McCabe shifted toward Ikard as he if were going to join the questioning. Ikard's eyes widened and his nostrils flared.

"All right. *All right!* I slept with Sylvia. Is that a crime?"

"No, that's a start."

Holt tilted her chair back and smiled as if she knew a few secrets Ikard didn't. Then she toyed with her pencil and stared at the barista while he squirmed.

McCabe had not seen her interrogation style until Sylvia Cole was murdered. Up until then, neither he nor his deputy had anything more taxing to do than lock up a few drunks or locate somebody's dog who had slipped his leash in the park and had run off to look for scraps behind Stacked.

Holt suddenly banged her chair forward. Ikard jumped as if she'd fired her service revolver.

"I want to know everything you did the night Sylvia was murdered. And don't you dare leave out one thing."

"I didn't do anything. Okay? I slept with her and then I left."

"What time did you get there?"

"I don't remember. Okay? It was sometime after dark."

"You didn't look at your watch? Check your clock when you left The Grind?"

"Living by the clock is what old folks do. That's the reason I came to Shutter Lake to open my coffee shop. The laid-back atmosphere."

McCabe studied their suspect. Now that Ikard had confessed to sleeping with Sylvia, he was more confident, slightly more relaxed.

Holt needed to tighten up. She was about to lose him.

"What time did you leave Sylvia's?" she said.

"I don't know. About an hour after I got there. Maybe less."

"Was that right after you killed her?"

Bingo! Ikard looked like he'd just wet his pants.

"No. *God,* no. I would *never* have killed Sylvia. She was a beautiful woman. A good person. We made love and I left. That's all. I swear."

Holt let him sweat a while, gave him time to wonder whether she believed him.

"Was anybody else there that night besides you and Sylvia?"

"No. Of course not! It was just the two of us."

"You don't sound too sure about that."

"I'm positive." Ikard pulled a handkerchief from his pocket and wiped his face. "I've got a stomach virus. I wonder if I could have some water."

McCabe stepped to the door and Officer Trask, who had been stationed just outside, handed him a bottle of Artesian water. Another perk of keeping law and order in Shutter Lake. Everything at the police department was the best money could buy, including the bottled water.

Holt let Ikard take a sip, and then she pounced. "Now, tell me again who else you saw at Sylvia Cole's the night you killed her."

"How many times do I have to tell you? I did *not* kill Sylvia! She was alive and happy when I left."

"Are you sure?"

"Yes, I'm sure. The last time I saw Sylvia she was fine."

"Where was she?"

"On her bed." Ikard guzzled his water.

"Ikard, look at me." Holt leaned closer and softened her voice. "What else did you see or hear that night?"

"I've already told you. *Nothing.*" He finished his water then set it on the table between them. "That's all I know."

Every good detective knows when to end an interrogation.

Holt stood up.

"You're free to go. But don't leave town."

After Ikard left, they both shouldered out of their jackets.

"He lied." Holt said.

"Which part?"

"I don't know. But I can tell you one thing. I'm going to find out."

"Not tonight, I hope."

"No, McCabe. Not tonight. You need your beauty sleep."

"Yeah, well, what are you planning to do? Sit in the pumpkin patch and hope the Great Pumpkin shows up?"

"Cute. Just get your butt home and let me worry about what I do."

"I've got one thing to say about that."

"What?"

"It had better not be illegal."

"Trust me on that, McCabe."

What else could he do? Laney Holt didn't know it, but she was the only thing that stood between him and absolute disgrace.

Chapter Eleven

What had she done? What had she done? What had she done?

The hounds of hell were closing in on Heidi. First, the law and that has-been reporter had been nosing around her shop all morning and then Troy Duval had guessed her secret.

The bitch was dead — murdered, they said - the day after Heidi had delivered her lethal gift.

Heidi didn't have any idea whether she'd killed Sylvia Cole. Or partially killed her, and somebody else finished her off.

For that matter, she hadn't seen that cute exchange student either. How long had it been? Lately, Heidi couldn't remember shit.

Josie Rodriguez worked part time down at Sparkle and had a big sweet tooth, that much she remembered. She used to pop by Batter Up nearly every day for a cupcake or a doughnut with icing. She was partial to chocolate. What if Sylvia had carried the whole box of cupcakes to Sparkle? What if Josie had eaten one of Heidi's poisonous treats with chocolate delight frosting? There'd been enough rat poison in one cupcake to kill three like Josie. She was model-thin.

And what about that cute guy Sylvia had brought into Batter Up? He was new in town, and after that one time, Heidi hadn't seen him, either. What if Sylvia had given him a lethal butter cream cupcake?

Griff McCabe and Laney Holt were nobody's fools. The cops would have gone through Sylvia's house with a fine-toothed comb, dusting for fingerprints, bagging evidence. Heidi's cupcakes might already be down at Shutter Lake PD. The chief of police and his deputy might already know she'd laced them with rat poison.

Even worse. What if some fool cop down there had decided to eat the cupcakes rather than treat them like evidence?

Oh, what had Heidi done? They'd lock her up and throw away the key. She'd become more notorious than Lizzie Borden with her lethal ax.

There was only one thing to do. Something she should have done right after the bitch was killed.

But how could Heidi get near Sylvia's house when the cops

were in and out at all hours, day and night? Still, she had to take the chance. Otherwise, she was going to fall dead of a heart attack right in the middle of making German chocolate frosting. Or even worse, in the middle of a hot vat of oil with her doughnuts.

Heidi flung open her closet door and dressed all in black then sat down with the bag of doughnuts she'd brought from her shop to wait until midnight. That seemed the right time to her. Surely the cops wouldn't be at Sylvia's house then. Shutter Lake was not a busy metropolis. Most folks would be in bed at the witching hour.

Night was a long time coming and midnight, even longer. Heidi ate the rest of the doughnuts then grabbed a penlight and her Halloween mask, the replica of a smiling Hillary Clinton on the campaign trail. Then she drove to Olive Tree Lane.

When she entered Sylvia's street, she turned off her car lights and coasted till she was one block down. She'd meant to park two blocks away but all that sugar had stolen her wind. She pocketed her car keys and penlight, then put on her mask and crept through the shadows provided by shrubs and trees. Shutter Lake prided itself on being green, but Heidi didn't think skulking unseen through the dark had been the intention of the city's founding fathers.

Yellow crime tape surrounded Sylvia's house. Heidi's legs weren't long enough to climb over without fear of breaking the tape. She was forced to crawl under like a snake.

The last time Heidi had slithered she'd been seventy-five pounds lighter and a whole lot younger. Her black long-sleeved tee caught on one of Sylvia's infernal rose bushes. The tearing sound rivaled a buzz saw, at least to Heidi's heightened senses.

Now she'd left evidence of breaking and entering for the police to find.

Heidi turned on her penlight and searched until she saw the incriminating black swatch attached to thorn. She grabbed it and stuffed it in her pocket and wondered if this night would never end. What if the cops were stationed inside the house in case the killer came back?

Or what if a really evil murderer was already in the house trying to retrieve his own evidence?

Heidi could barely think lying down and she was getting an awful cramp in her right leg. She gingerly shook it and....oh God, what was that shadow outside Sylvia's window?

She tried to remain calm but her own breathing sounded like one of Brenda Lockhart's racehorses coming in last at the Kentucky Derby.

Get a hold of yourself, Heidi Udall.

Suddenly the shadow separated itself from Sylvia's windowsill and leaped toward Heidi. She lost her bladder control and her fragile hold on sanity at the same time. Screaming, she scrambled backward toward the protection of the rose bush just as the cat streaked by.

Now she'd done it.

She lay in the dirt for five minutes, expecting each one to be the moment she got hauled off in handcuffs. When nothing happened except an uncomfortable wetness traveling down the leg of her trousers, Heidi decided to press on. What choice did she have?

She knew and resented every inch of Sylvia's house, inside and out. Heidi's money had helped pay for all that ostentation. She wasn't sorry one bit that she'd tried to poison the bitch.

Anger propelled her to Sylvia's bedroom window, but it was not enough to get her over the too-tall windowsill. Heidi had to drag a chair off the front porch. Wrought iron, of all things. Every second of this added complication increased her chances of getting caught.

Heidi stepped on the chair and for an awful moment thought it would collapse under her weight. But no, she was finally teetering on top, finally close enough to force open the window. Heidi stiffened, waiting for an alarm. Thank goodness, all was quiet.

Inch by inch she hefted a leg over the sill. So far, so good.

Heidi eased her other foot up and the chair toppled with a crash that sounded like Armageddon. Heidi was left astraddle the sill. Unfortunately, her seat was not steady. No matter how much she waved her arms and prayed for balance, she catapulted into Sylvia's bedroom as if she'd been shot from a cannon.

Her head banged on Sylvia's bedpost, nearly knocking her silly, and Heidi didn't even want to think about the state of her backside. It had hit the floor at the same velocity of a Talladega racecar crashing into the wall.

She lay there groaning. If she could get down to the morgue, she'd beat Sylvia Cole 'til she was black and blue.

Well, she probably already was.

Taking small comfort in the thought, Heidi finally hefted her aching body off the floor and limped into the kitchen. It was stark black in the house, but Heidi knew this kitchen almost as well as her own. She had no trouble spotting the refrigerator. Her biggest trouble came in shuffling toward it without yelping in pain.

She stood there a while working up her courage, and then she opened the refrigerator door.

Heidi nearly wept. The cupcakes were there. All twelve of them. Untouched.

She was so relieved she grabbed a buttercream for herself. It was halfway to her mouth before she remembered it was laced with enough poison to fell a horse.

Chapter Twelve

Saturday, October 13

It was dark and cold and the incessant rain only added to Julia's misery.

He was coming. She could hear his footsteps in the hall.

Would today be her last?

She woke with her heart pounding and the sound of rain beating against the window. Her nightlight cast shadows on the blue walls and the face of her bedside clock glowed, bringing the numbers into sharp relief. It was six a.m. and she was in her own bed in Shutter Lake.

Usually she'd turn over and go back to sleep. She'd wait until a decent hour to get out of bed and start her day. But events of the past few days wouldn't let her sleep. She threw on her robe and padded through her house barefoot, following the glow of her nightlights into her kitchen.

Julia popped a K-cup into her Keurig then pulled open her blackout curtains over the sink. The rain had already slowed to a drizzle. By the time the crowd started gathering on the town square, the sun would be out. California weather was not as exciting or as varied as Chicago's but it had its advantages.

Julia toasted an English muffin, slathered it with cream cheese then took it and her coffee cup into her office. She turned on the lamp on her desk then powered up her computer and typed her interview with Katherine Windermere for the *Firefly*.

Even if the article would never win an award, never be cited on the evening news, Julia didn't skimp on quality. She'd come to love Shutter Lake. Didn't its readers deserve the best from her?

She'd do a follow-up article for next week's edition after today's symphony on the park. A list of big donors – everybody loved seeing their generosity spread all over the local newspaper – a few quotes from attendees, a description of the food. Julia's readers loved anything about food, particularly the exotic fare Katherine

Windermere provided at all her events. And make no mistake - this fund-raiser was Katherine's event.

By the time Julia had emailed her article to the newspaper office then showered and dressed, it was time to pick up Rick. Though she'd have preferred walking – she loved seeing the way a rain-washed world glistened in the sun – she took her car. She and Rick still had much ground to cover, and driving made her feel more in charge. Yesterday, sitting in the passenger side with Rick at the wheel had felt too much like being sucked into the past.

~

Rick was sitting at a wicker table on the front porch of the B&B on Main, holding a huge mug of coffee and chatting with the owner. Brenda Lockhart sat in a wicker rocking chair nearby with her booted feet resting on a paisley covered wicker ottoman. You could see her neon yellow shirt all the way to the Pacific. She'd topped that off with a fringed leather vest. The only thing missing was her cowboy hat. Julia had no doubt she'd don that before the symphony.

"Well, look what the cat dragged in!" Brenda waved a hand covered in diamonds. "Make yourself comfortable. I was just telling Rick how I came to have horses descended from Seabiscuit."

"Kentucky bred, wasn't he?"

"He was. You know your horses, girl." Brenda waved a hand toward a wicker rocking chair. "Sit down. I'll get you a cup of coffee."

"Thank you, but no. We really have to be going."

"I know that feeling. I used to be young." Brenda winked then waved at them as they descended her front porch steps and headed across the street where the town square was already filling up with people.

As soon as they were out of earshot, Julia said, "Did you find out anything from her this morning?"

"Adler didn't stay at the B&B."

"That's strange. The B&B's the only place in Shutter Lake to stay. Maybe he stayed nearby."

"I already checked Grass Valley, Rocklin and Sacramento."

"Maybe he stayed in San Francisco. We can check that out after we leave here."

They crossed the street and were immediately immersed in the town's annual fund-raising gala. Overnight the town square had been transformed. A huge banner across the front of the temporary stage proclaimed ANNUAL SHUTTER LAKE BENEFIT CONCERT. A microphone sat in the center of the stage and the perimeter sprouted with mums in fall colors plus sheaves of wheat and pumpkins that showed Katherine Windermere's touch.

A two-hundred-thousand-dollar concert grand piano from the Windermere Center for the Arts had been moved across the street and dominated the stage. Folding chairs for the orchestra made a semi-circle around the impressive piano.

Several feet from the stage was a small tent bearing the sign SUPPORT THE ARTS. Volunteer sat behind a long folding table collecting money that would be used to keep the arts center and all its programs running.

In front of the stage, folding chairs cordoned off with velvet rope had been set up for the dignitaries. Nearby, vendors sold balloons, ice cream and lemonade. A massive white tent stenciled with the lettering HELENE'S CATERING OF SAN FRANCISCO occupied the east quadrant of the square.

A quick glance showed that all of Shutter Lake's most prominent citizens were in attendance, with one notable exception - Connie and Vernon Bradshaw. Not surprising since their son Vinn had only recently been incarcerated in the city's jail, accused of murder. Even though he'd been cleared of all charges, it would take a while for the Bradshaws to pick up the pieces and move forward.

"Julia?" Rick put a hand on her elbow. "Where do you want to start?"

"We might find out more if we separate. Sometimes people feel like you're ganging up on them if it's two against one."

"That sounds reasonable. Where and when do you want to meet?"

"In front of the stage when the orchestra starts tuning up. It will be a while."

"All right. See you then."

Rick strode in the direction of the catering tent and Julia scanned the crowd. Mayor Jessup stood off to the left of the stage, surrounded by city council members. He always made a speech at these fundraisers. Would he bring up the murder that was on everybody's minds or would he try to lead the town into a false sense of security?

"Julia!"

She turned to see Heidi Udall heading her way, flanked by two sweet-faced, earnest looking women in straw hats. All three of them carried ice cream cones.

"Heidi, how are you?"

Not too well, judging by appearances. Heidi had limped toward her, and now that she was close Julia could see she'd used too much pancake makeup in an attempt to cover a bruise on the side of her forehead.

"Fabulous! I couldn't be better! I'd like you to meet my dear friends from church, Martha Wright and Sally Hanson. Girls, this is the famous writer from the *Firefly*."

What had gotten into the woman? There was not a hint of irony in Heidi's introduction. And why, all of a sudden, was she acting as if Julia were her best friend? Was she gloating because she'd stonewalled Julia and Rick yesterday at Batter Up? Or had her ill temper of the previous day had nothing at all to do with being questioned and everything to do with a lonely woman simply having a bad day?

Maybe her watery eyes had been due to weeping.

"Oh!" Heidi suddenly turned her attention to the striking silver-haired couple near the fountain. "I see Katherine! I've got to run tell her how fabulous this event is."

Heidi limped off toward Katherine and Quentin Windermere, leaving a trail of jungle gardenia perfume and melting ice cream. Julia might have followed at a discreet distance to find out what she was up to, but her attention was drawn toward another couple.

Yolanda and Zion Cole. The dead girl's parents.

She wasn't surprised they'd come. The Coles were staunch supporters of the arts and a backbone of city. They'd borne their daughter's murder with grace, attending every press conference at City Hall and offering a handsome reward for information leading to the capture of her killer.

Julia had not spoken to them since Sylvia's murder, an unforgivable lapse on her part. She was headed that way when she saw Nolan Ikard, skulking along behind the Coles. His shoulders were hunched and his face was a study in sorrow and rage. Occasionally his gaze darted in every direction, as if he were afraid he was being followed.

Not surprising considering Laney and McCabe had been on stakeout last night to catch him.

Julia dropped back to observe three of the major players in Sylvia Cole's murder, the victim's parents and the victim's suspected killer. The latter was an assumption, but she was on pretty solid ground with it.

Zion Cole had his arm around his wife, probably as much to support her as to comfort. Fatigue and grief etched her face, and every once in a while she stumbled against her husband. He would pat her hand and lean down to murmur something into her ear.

Every time the Coles paused, so did Nolan Ikard. Strange.

Even stranger was the way Ikard watched them, particularly Zion. Julia couldn't decipher the look. Was it fear? Hatred? Or merely the confusion of someone who'd known Sylvia well and didn't know how to approach her parents to express his sympathy?

Suddenly the microphone blared to life, a stage hand tapping it and saying, "Testing, testing."

Mayor Jessup took the stage while Zion and Yolanda, Katherine and Quentin and most of the city council members slid into the reserved seats.

Chief of Police Griff McCabe moved in to stand close to the cordoned off area of dignitaries, his white shirt immaculate, his jeans crisp and his sunglasses partially hiding a face that was a bit haggard. Beside him Laney kept a tight rein on her emotions, her face showing nothing but a quiet confidence.

She was good at that. In spite of everything that had happened to her in Los Angeles.

Julia watched her friend until Laney looked up and gave her a little nod.

We've got this covered, that small gesture said. *We will persevere.*

"Ladies and gentlemen," the mayor said, "we've come here today because we believe in the future of Shutter Lake. We believe we've built the best and most progressive town in California, and we intend to keep it that way!"

He waited for the burst of applause to die down. "In spite of the grief we all share with Zion and Yolanda Cole over the untimely death of their daughter and one of this town's finest citizens, we will not neglect our civic duties. And we will not neglect the arts!"

The applause this time was thunderous and prolonged. The mayor moved on to introduce Katherine and Quentin, who came to the microphone where Katherine made a plea for donations to help support the many and varied programs offered at Windermere Center for the Arts. She complimented the gathering on their continuing support that had allowed a town as small as Shutter Lake to maintain a full orchestra since the city was first incorporated.

She ended her plea by saying, "Your generous donations help keep the arts alive, and art is the very soul of a community."

After his wife had finished her speech, Quentin escorted her from the stage. Mayor Jessup came back to the microphone to exhort the town to give generously.

"We have a list of donors who have already made substantial pledges," he added. Then he read some of the major contributions. Thousand-dollar donations had come in from the Wine and Cheese House, Johnny's, the B&B on Main, Dr. Ana Perez at the Shutter Lake Medical Clinic. Ray Jones over at The Rabbit Hole had donated five thousand. But the biggest donation so far had come from Zion and Yolanda Cole.

"Twenty-five thousand dollars," the mayor said, and the entire city council stood to give the Coles a standing ovation.

Yolanda remained seated during the applause, but Zion stood up and turned to face the crowd, his slight nod in their direction an acknowledgment that he was with them still. Then, unexpectedly, he strode toward the stage.

A wave of excitement stirred through the crowd. Even Julia got goose bumps when he joined Mayor Jessup at the microphone.

"Mayor, if I may?" he said, and Thomas Jessup relinquished his place on center stage. Zion put his hand on the microphone as if he needed it to steady himself, and then he leaned forward to study the gathering.

It was an electrifying moment. Zion was an imposing figure, a tall handsome man with riveting blue eyes and silver hair. His long and successful career as an investment analyst had honed his communication skills. He knew the power of the dramatic pause.

In that long, searching silence you could hear the fearful beat of your own heart.

"My friends…"

A palpable sigh went through the crowd. They could relax

now. Zion was one of their own. He'd just said so.

"I'm part of the very fabric of this town. Along with my beautiful wife, I'm going to make every effort to remain active in the civic and social life of Shutter Lake. We will not let our daughter's death keep us from civic duty."

The cheers from the crowd were heartfelt and prolonged.

"We encourage you to do the same. We challenge you to match our contribution to the arts of Shutter Lake." He held up his hand to stop the applause. "Before you rush over to the tent to make your donations, I have one more thing to say to you...Help me find Sylvia's killer. I will give anyone with information that leads to this monster's arrest two and half million dollars."

Shocked silence rippled through the crowd, followed by an explosion of excitement. Zion had just raised the reward money by half a million dollars. And that was after doubling it only days ago.

He left the stage as abruptly as he'd come. A few people rushed toward him, but Griff McCabe held them back while Zion gathered his wife and moved off toward the east side of the square.

Were they headed toward the catering tent? Julia headed in that direction. Here was her follow-up story. *Zion and Yolanda Cole – Biggest Donors for the Arts.*

Julia would leave the reward money out of her article. She wouldn't mention murder or the name of the murder victim. Nor the very odd fact that Zion's daughter had been found murdered on October fourth and the huge reward was still unclaimed.

Though she could feel the old familiar itch for the big story, Julia refocused. She no longer covered the crime beat.

And she didn't want to.

Or did she?

Mouth-watering smells from the catering tent wafted her way. Blue crab, shrimp scampi, chicken cordon bleu. Her talent for identifying food by smell told her just how long she'd been away from the mean streets of Chicago and in the safe kitchens of Shutter Lake.

She pushed the thought from her mind as she caught up with Zion and Yolanda.

"Mr. and Mrs. Cole..." They turned in her direction, Yolanda welcoming and Zion skeptical. "I wonder if I might have a word. I'm Julia Ford from the *Firefly* and the *Sacramento Bee.*"

"I know who you are," Zion said. "What is this about?"

"First, I wanted to offer my sincere sympathy. I'm sorry I haven't had a chance to do it sooner."

"My dear. It's never too late," Yolanda said. "Sylvia spoke highly of you."

Julia was surprised. Her only personal contact with Sylvia Cole had been a feature she'd done on Sparkle after Sylvia had won the Chamber of Commerce's business of the year award. She'd been cordial and forthcoming, even charming. But there had been nothing in the encounter that would lead Julia to believe Sylvia would mention her later, particularly in glowing terms.

"Thank you, Mrs. Cole. That's very kind of you to tell me."

"I trust her judgment completely." Yolanda's face went white as she realized her error.

"You've upset my wife." Zion wrapped his arm around Yolanda's shoulder. "I think you'd better leave."

"No, no, Zion. I want to talk to her." She reached out and grabbed Julia's hand. "None of Sylvia's friends will talk to me. They're scared to."

"Yolanda, you don't need to do this."

"Yes, I do, Zion. I *do.*" She still clung almost desperately to Julia's hand. "Tell me anything you know about my girl. I need to hear from her friends so I can keep her alive." She released Julia and put her hand over her heart. "In *here.*"

"Sylvia was beloved in this town, Mrs. Cole. Everywhere I go, someone has something nice to say about her."

Only two people, actually. Ray down at the Rabbit Hole, and his motives were suspect, and Shonda at The Grind, who was just a scared kid. But Sylvia's mother didn't have to know.

"You don't know how much it means to hear you say that."

"Your daughter was kind to everybody. Even strangers in town." Julia's conscience pricked her, but she told herself she could do this without further upsetting Yolanda and Zion Cole. "She even took the time to show a friend of mine around Shutter Lake. Perhaps you know him? Evan Adler."

Zion cleared his throat. "Never heard of him. We need to go, Yolanda."

"Just a *minute.* If I can't take a minute to talk about my daughter, then you can just go home without me, Zion. I can hitch a ride."

"Now, Yolanda…"

"Sylvia is *dead... murdered.*" Yolanda's chest heaved. "And I want to talk about her." Her voice broke apart and she began to wail.

Zion shot Julia a look of such pure venom she took a step backward. Then he tightened his arm around Yolanda and bent over to talk softly while he trotted her off.

Julia wanted to kick herself. Her own experience with the Jack o' Lantern killer should have taught her that a murder leaves behind more than the untimely dead. It leaves fragile living victims – grieving family and friends, and yes, sometimes even survivors - who should be treated with great care.

"Julia!" Rick waved then strode toward her. "The orchestra is tuning up and you weren't there."

"I got distracted."

"Have you learned anything?"

"Nothing useful. You?"

"Unfortunately, no."

Across the square the Shutter Lake Symphony launched into Beethoven's magnificent "Coriolan Overture, Op. 62." For a moment Julia stood quietly, letting herself get lost in the beauty of music. Then she laced her arm through Rick's.

"We need a break. Let's get some food and then go over to the stage and enjoy the music."

Chapter Thirteen

Quentin Windermere's greatest satisfaction in the annual fundraiser for the arts was not in seeing how much money the town donated. If they didn't give a penny, he'd make certain the arts never died in Shutter Lake. No, his biggest pleasure was in watching his wife enjoy the fruits of their civic labors.

Today she was off-kilter. Ludwig Van Beethoven was one of her most beloved composers. She was particularly fond of "The Coriolan Overture." Usually she'd listen with her eyes closed and her face filled with rapture. It pained him to see her tense and staring, barely aware of the violins and the cello, two of her favorite instruments.

It was the murder. And the sight of Sylvia's grieving parents. Katherine was the gentlest, most sensitive soul on earth. How it must have hurt her to see Yolanda and Zion trying to carry on.

Even Quentin, who knew Sylvia's dark side, had been moved almost to tears when Zion got up on the stage. He'd exhorted the town to match his more-than-generous donation, and then he'd started talking about his dead daughter.

Nine days, and the killer was still at large. Where would it all end?

The overture ended to thunderous applause. When Joseph Klein, music director, came to the podium to announce the next number, Katherine shot Quentin a helpless look.

He leaned close and whispered, "What, darling?"

"I don't think I can stand this any longer."

Alarm skittered through him. What on earth was Katherine talking about? Klein was onstage telling the origins of "Variaciones Concertantes, Op. 23" by twentieth century composer Alberto Ginastera, a joyful piece that usually had his wife dancing around their house, barefoot.

Was she that upset by seeing the Coles?

An even more horrible alternative presented itself. What if she'd somehow unearthed his dirty little secret? What if she'd discovered that their entire life in Shutter Lake had been built on lies?

"You love Ginastera. Are you sure you want to leave?"

"Positive. I'll make my apologies to Klein later."

There was a small stir when he and Katherine left their seats. And was it any wonder? In all their years in Shutter Lake, they'd never walked out in the middle of a performance. Of any kind. Symphony. Ballet. Theater. Poetry reading. They loved them all.

Today's exit was unheard of.

Quentin hoped people would blame it on the current unrest in town. He'd even be happy to have them blame it on age. *Poor old Quentin and Katherine*, they'd say. *They're getting too old to run the arts community. They need to step down and let someone younger take over.*

He almost wished someone would, but who would it be? He had no son or daughter to follow in his footsteps, no protégé in business who shared his intense sense of civic duty and responsibility to Shutter Lake.

Maybe it was time to start mentoring someone who could take the helm of Windermere Center for the Arts. Josie would be the perfect choice. But she was down in Venezuela on some wild notion or other. Katherine knew more about it than he did.

Thankfully, he and Katherine were able to slip through the square almost unnoticed. Nearly everybody there was crowded around the stage listening to the symphony, some in lawn chairs, some on quilts, a few sitting in the grass under the shade of trees.

If Quentin could turn back the clock, he'd have spent less time making money and more time attending to the things that matter. Loving his wife. Building a family.

They could have adopted. *Should* have adopted.

Today they might have been any other ordinary couple, sitting on a quilt watching their grandchildren dance in the grass to the sound of great music.

When they got to their car, Quentin was sweating and his heart was beating too fast. Was he going to start having health problems? Is that what was going on? Or was it worry?

He turned on the air conditioner without asking Katherine. She glanced his way, her eyebrow lifted.

"Are you okay?" she asked.

"Fine. It's you I'm worried about. What's going on in that pretty head of yours?"

"I just want to go. I think we've done enough for today, don't you?"

He maneuvered out of the parking lot and headed home, glad to have something to do, glad he'd decided to do the driving today and didn't have to wait for Sykes to pick them up.

"Do you want to go to the lake? A sail might do us both some good."

"No. I want to go home."

This was serious. Katherine loved the water as much as he did. Maybe even more. Sometimes he went just to please her. He'd much rather be home puttering around the garden in his roses than sailing on Shutter Lake, or God forbid, driving all the way to San Francisco and going out in the yacht.

But he wasn't about to disappoint her. She was everything to him.

Everything.

His thoughts circled like mad squirrels as he drove. Maybe he needed to see Dr. Perez. She could give him something for stress.

Maybe Katherine needed to see her. What if her unusual slump was a sign of illness? What if it was cancer or some equally horrible illness that would take her from him?

She was all he had. He'd die if he lost her.

"Quentin." Katherine touched his arm. "What's Maria's car doing here?"

"Beats me."

He turned the car into his driveway and parked beside a fourteen-year-old Chevrolet that looked as if it couldn't make the next corner, let alone the drive from Grass Valley to Shutter Lake.

Jimmy Sykes hurried out to open Katherine's door and put the car in the garage. Quentin left the keys in the ignition.

"Sir, Maria Rodriguez is inside."

"Did she say what she wants?"

"No, sir. She's waiting in the kitchen."

"The kitchen?"

"I told her to wait in the family room, sir, but she insisted she'd be more comfortable in the kitchen."

"Oh, for goodness sake, you two! Stop making a federal case of it. Maria and I have coffee in the kitchen all the time." Katherine flounced past them and into the house.

Quentin was so happy to see her spirit improved he almost stopped worrying about what was in her craw. He stayed outside long enough to tell Jimmy to go ahead and take the rest of the day off.

They wouldn't need him this afternoon. Frankly, Quentin looked forward to a few minutes in his own home with nobody there except his wife. Maybe he could find out what was eating Katherine.

His own spirits restored, he whistled a Broadway show tune as he walked into the house. Classical music was well and good, but every now and then a man needed music with a funky beat and lyrics you could sing.

When he walked into the kitchen, his tune suffered an abrupt death.

Maria Rodriguez was huddled in her chair sobbing while Katherine alternately wiped the woman's round face with a dishcloth and stroked her salt and pepper hair.

"Oh, Quentin." Katherine raced to him and caught his lapels. "Josie is missing."

"Missing? How could that be?"

"I don't know. Maria thinks something is horribly wrong. She believes she's never going to hear from Josie again."

"Why didn't she let us know sooner?" Katherine shook her head, and Quentin strode to the distraught woman's chair to kneel beside her. "Maria? What's going on? Do you feel like talking to me?"

"Oh, Mr. Windermere. I didn't want to worry you. The cops are asking questions and Josie's boss is dead and I'm waiting to hear from my daughter. She was too young to go to Venezuela by herself. It's my fault she's gone."

Quentin tamped down his own sense of foreboding. There were many explanations why a girl as young as Josie wouldn't report to her mother after a flight to Venezuela. Excitement. Reconnecting with an old boyfriend. Forgetfulness. But to wait so long? Over two months?

Even with a country in chaos, relatives without phones, Josie would have found some way to contact Maria. She was not the kind of girl to worry her mother, but maybe she thought someone else in the family had reported to Maria.

"Now, Maria, before we all go jumping to conclusions, let's go over this puzzle piece by piece. Are you all right with that?"

"Okay."

"Did she call you when she first arrived in Venezuela?"

"No. I waited and waited."

"Did you call the family to see if she arrived?"

"They have no phone. Things are bad down there and his neighbor with the phone is away." A fresh torrent of weeping bent her almost double.

Quentin tamped down his growing concern as he patted her hand. His wife hovered over Maria making soothing sounds.

"Katherine, darling, get her some water. We have to get to the bottom of this."

After Maria had downed half a glass of water, she said, "I'm okay now."

"You're sure?" Katherine stroked her hair. "You can lie down a while if you want, and Quentin can talk to you later." Her fierce glance dared her husband to contradict her.

"No. I need to find my daughter." Maria drew a shaky breath. "Finally the neighbor returns and I hear from my brother. Josie was not on the plane."

The awful possibilities plus Quentin's own dirty past converged in his mind and almost brought him to his knees.

One hope stood between him and damnation – that Maria's disjointed account omitted one crucial fact. Josie had finally called her mother to explain why she didn't get on the plane and they'd had a big argument that resulted in more than two months of silence.

Any mother would worry over that.

"How long has it actually been since you heard from Josie?"

"Mr. Windermere, the last time I heard from Josie, she was going to leave for the airport with you."

~

They'd assured Maria they would do everything in their power to find her daughter, and she'd gone back to Grass Valley. Josie's mother had seemed calmer when she left. But Quentin was worried about his wife. Katherine couldn't quit crying.

He was on the sofa with his arms wrapped around her, and he didn't know what else to do. He'd reassured her in every way possible. He'd promised to hire a top-notch private eye and call in favors from everybody he knew in law enforcement, from the director of the FBI on down.

But she was inconsolable.

"Katherine, you're going to make yourself sick."

"All this is my fault."

"Darling, Josie's disappearance can't possibly be your fault. You were perfection with that girl. You're perfection with all our exchange students."

"No, Quentin. Listen to me. I should have gone with you to the airport, and I never should have lied to everybody and said that I did." She pushed herself up and stared at him. Her nose was red and mascara ran down her cheeks, but he'd never loved her more. She needed him, and that was enough. "I've lied about a lot of things."

"What things, darling?"

"For one thing, I don't like being on the water."

"Why, I thought you loved it!"

"I'd much rather be over there," she nodded to the grand piano, "playing Bach or sitting here with you reading a good book."

He kissed the top of her head. "That's not much of a lie."

She traced his cheekbones then hid her face against his shoulder. "I tried to hire a hacker to get into your account."

Quentin froze, watching helplessly as his entire house of cards tumbled down around them. If his wife had any misgivings about him, how long before they turned into an avalanche of doubt, mistrust and fear?

He'd been a fool to keep secrets from her.

"Quentin?" Katherine raised her head. "You're not mad at me?"

"Sweetheart, I could never be mad at you." He kissed her forehead then stood up and walked to the fireplace. "There's something I have to tell you. Something I should have told you a long time ago."

His wife was quiet while he told her about being young and brash and filled with foolhardy ideas. She stiffened her spine when he admitted to using what little charm he had to convince beautiful young women to star in pornographic movies. *His* pornographic movies. She wiped her tears and the mascara streaking her cheeks while he told her how he'd justified his films as tasteful porn because the money was pouring in. More money than he'd ever dreamed.

He explained that over time he had become immensely

wealthy…and grown a conscience. Besides, he'd met a woman who made him want to be his best self. They'd built a life that included taking in foreign students, ensuring their future. Quentin had believed he was making up for what he'd done, atoning for his sins.

By the time he'd finished baring his soul, Katherine's eyes were dry and both feet were planted on the floor. She was as composed as if she were listening to a book review on NPR.

Quentin had never known his own wife could be such a good actress. What was she thinking? Was she going to leave him now?

"Sylvia Cole unearthed my dirty past and was blackmailing me. So you see, Katherine, if anyone in this house is responsible for Josie's disappearance, it's me. Not you."

Katherine didn't move, didn't speak. Did she hate him? He could live if she walked out and made a life for herself that didn't include him and his sleazy past. But he didn't know how he could endure her hatred.

"I can never forgive myself for what I did, Katherine. It was unconscionable. I'd give everything I own if I could turn back the clock and choose another path. The best I can do is try to find those women and make amends." Her silence broke his heart. Was hers breaking, too? "It's too much to expect your forgiveness."

"Oh, Quentin." Only two words, but her shattered voice spoke volumes.

"I'm going to call Griff McCabe. It's the only right thing to do. He needs to know about Josie's disappearance, and he needs to know that Sylvia was blackmailing me."

"No!"

The strength of her denial startled Quentin.

"I'm through with lying, Katherine. I'm going to tell Chief McCabe everything, including my own sordid past. I'll tell him you had no knowledge of it and nothing to do with it."

"Please don't do that, Quentin. You'll be arrested."

He went weak at the knees. She still cared.

"The lies stop now. I'll call our lawyer. He'll be there when we talk to McCabe."

"Please, please, *please.*" Katherine jumped off the sofa and wrapped her arms around him, buried her head on his shoulder. "I can't stand to see you humiliated in front of the whole town."

As he closed his arms around her, his gratitude was immeasurable.

"You're the one I'm worried about, Katherine. My slime will spill all over you. I can't bear to think about that."

They stood in front of the stone fireplace, locked together in love and grief.

Finally she said, "We'll call Julia."

"Julia? Why on earth do you say that?"

"She's an investigative journalist. She'll know what to do." She gave him a watery smile. "I know this is silly, but she's also a pianist. You can trust a woman who plays the piano."

Quentin was willing to call the Pillsbury Dough Boy if it would make Katherine happy.

Chapter Fourteen

The Shutter Lake Symphony Orchestra was just finishing Beethoven's "Piano Concerto No. 4 in G Major" when Julia's phone vibrated. She glanced at the screen. Katherine Windermere.

She mouthed the name to Rick then slipped away from the crowd and took the call. Katherine was crying and impossible to understand.

What on earth was going on?

"I didn't get that. Could you repeat it?"

"Just come to the house, Julia. Please come."

"We'll be right there." Julia motioned to Rick then dropped her phone into her bag and slung it over her shoulder.

"What was that all about?"

"We'll find out soon enough."

Julia was sorry to leave the town square. For a few hours the sounds of music, the smell of good food and the easy laughter had made her forget a killer was on the loose in Shutter Lake.

If she closed her eyes and let her mind drift with the fall breeze, she could imagine it was a year ago where the most exciting thing to happen in the town had been Heidi Udall introducing her new Chocolate Delight cupcakes at Batter Up.

Heidi and her friends were back at the ice cream stand when Julia and Rick passed by.

"Are you leaving before the concert's over?" Heidi called.

Julia was torn between pretending she hadn't heard and being polite. Manners won. Thanks to Rachel. Sometimes a friendly word makes the difference between a lousy day and good one. One of her mother's many truisms.

"I'm afraid so," Julia told her. "Duty calls."

"That's too bad. They'll be raffling the door prizes soon. I've donated two dozen cupcakes from Batter Up."

"Chocolate Delight I hope."

"I used a variety of my specialties. That's one of them."

"Great. See you."

Julia waved and lengthened her stride. Still, Heidi called after her. "Have a good day!"

Rick matched Julia's steps and caught up to her. "Is that the same surly woman I saw in Batter Up only yesterday?"

"I don't know. Maybe Sylvia came back and took over Heidi's body."

He shot her a look but, thank goodness, he didn't comment. Good. Julia was in no mood to soul search.

She scanned the crowd one last time before they left the square. It was significantly smaller than earlier this morning. Nolan Ikard was nowhere to be found, and of course, the Coles and the Windermeres were gone.

The owner of The Rabbit Hole was leaving the square while Dana Perkins and Ana Perez were arriving. Dana smiled broadly and waved. Julia lifted her hand to wave back when she saw Thomas Jessup waving and striding in the direction of Shutter Lake's most popular red-head.

What was up with that? Julia planned to find out, even if she had to call another emergency girls' night out at Dana's house.

"Where'd you go, Julia?"

"Off to Neverland, I guess."

On the way to her car Julia got her head back in the game and told Rick what little she knew about Katherine's call. There was no sense speculating. She was used to heading blind toward a source.

A shiver passed through her. Something about Katherine's call felt like the old days. She just hoped this tip didn't turn out to be as horrific as her last one.

~

Quentin Windermere met them at the door.

He didn't even look like the same man Julia had seen earlier on the town square. His face was pinched and his eyes looked hollow. In addition, his slightly lifted eyebrow made it clear he'd expected Julia to arrive alone.

She introduced the men, making certain she tagged Rick as Special Agent Patrick Richardson.

In spite of his appearance and the shock of having an FBI agent on his doorstep, Quentin fell right into the casual grace that always put people at ease.

"Thank you for coming so quickly. I hope this is not a terrible inconvenience for you."

"Not at all." Julia and Rick followed him into the family room where Katherine sat on the sofa with her bare feet tucked under. She was pale-faced and barely composed

"Thank you for coming," she said. "Do sit down."

Julia and Rick took chairs flanking the fireplace and facing the sofa. Quentin slid into place beside his wife and put his arm around her shoulders.

"Julia, we've asked you here because both of us, particularly Katherine, have great confidence in your judgment and your discretion."

"I never reveal my sources, if that's what you're saying."

"Oh, for goodness sake, Quentin! Stop tiptoeing around. We are worried sick about Josie. Her mother Maria hasn't heard from her since before she left for Venezuela, two and a half months ago."

Julia's stomach clenched. Josie missing and Sylvia dead. Her gut told her there had to be a connection. But what? How many more young women would vanish or be murdered before they found out?

Images of the beautiful Hispanic teenager tumbled through her mind. She wondered whether the Windermeres knew something she and Rick did not. Or did they simply know that Josie never got on the plane to Venezuela?

Katherine shrugged off her husband's arm. "We've both made a complete mess of things. I've lied to everybody and I'm afraid those lies have caused untold harm." She leaned closer to Julia. "You see, I was never with my husband when he took Josie to the airport."

"Josie *did* go through security. I saw her. My wife thought she was doing the right thing when she said she was there, too. Katherine is the most straight-forward, honest woman I know."

Julia waited to see where the Windermere's story was leading. Sometimes questions could send a person's story in an entirely different direction than they'd intended. Especially the wrong questions.

Katherine dismissed her husband's remarks with a wave.

"Sylvia and Josie were close, very close. Things have been so awful ever since Josie suddenly decided to leave for Venezuela. Her poor mother waited and waited for a call that never came and then Sylvia was murdered."

Katherine paused to regain control of her emotions before she soldiered bravely on. "The police have been asking questions. Quentin took Josie to the airport, and I know how often wealthy, famous men become targets of the unscrupulous. I never believed Josie would do anything to harm him, but there might have been any number of people who would use her to destroy my husband. I simply wanted to back up his story, to protect him in case he got implicated in any way."

"My wife even tried to hire a hacker to prove my innocence in case somebody accused me of wrongdoing." He actually smiled at the idea of a software wizard being hacked. "She said you knew about that, Julia."

"I did."

She knew, too, that both Windermeres were telling the truth. There was not a single facial tic or alteration of body language to suggest they were spinning lies.

She and Rick both remained quiet while the couple told of Maria Rodriguez's visit and alternately shared details that shivered Julia's soul. Visions of finding the teenager holed up somewhere in California with unsuitable friends or a boyfriend vanished. The hope of a finding a forgetful girl neglecting her filial duty was replaced by the very real possibility that Josie Rodriguez had come to a bad end.

The Windermeres finished their story then caught each other's hands and held on tight. Anyone who knew a thing about human nature could see grief and remorse written all over them.

Rick telegraphed his thoughts to Julia with a glance. *These are your friends. I'm backing off.*

They'd always been able to read each other, even in the beginning. How easy it was to fall back into old patterns. Too easy.

"What was she wearing when you last saw her?"

Quentin shrugged. Julia hadn't expected him to know. She was just glad he hadn't picked up the subtext. That was not the kind of question you'd ask of a girl you thought you'd find frolicking with friends after days of stubborn silence. It's the kind you asked when you were afraid you might find a body.

"Blue jeans, a white shirt and a red sweater," Katherine said. "With a silver poodle pin. She treasured that pin. Sylvia gave it to her."

"When was this? Do you recall?"

"It was just a few days before Josie left for Venezuela. Sylvia gave it to her as a little award for being Sparkle's most valued employee for that month. Josie *adored* the woman and was always asking her questions about starting a business. She planned to be just like Sylvia."

"How did Sylvia react to Josie's hero worship?"

"She tried to mentor all her girls down at Sparkle. Lately, though, she'd paid particular attention to Josie. I think she bought that pin to encourage her. She knew Josie wanted to get a poodle and start a pet grooming business after graduation." Katherine smiled at the memory. "I have no idea why she wanted that breed. But she talked incessantly about it."

"She'd even picked out a name," Quentin said. "Clarence. She finally wore us down with her talk. We'd promised to get her a registered standard poodle for graduation."

Julia relaxed as much as she could and let the Windermeres prattle on with information that had no bearing on Josie's disappearance. Their memories seemed to bring them a measure of comfort.

Finally she said, "We already knew Josie didn't get on the plane. We've been looking for her and Special Agent Evan Adler both."

A look of alarm crossed Quentin's face. Had his wife not told him they'd been there inquiring about Adler? Or was it the mention of a second FBI agent that struck a wrong chord with him?

Had Julia totally misjudged their innocence? It would be the first time she'd made that mistake. She'd followed a seemingly innocent promise of a tip for her story right into the hands of the Jack o' Lantern killer.

Julia shot Rick a signal. *Your turn.* She hoped he didn't notice that she was beginning to unravel.

"Katherine, have you remembered anything else about Agent Adler that would help us?"

She went very quiet, and once again, Julia mistrusted her own instincts. Was Katherine stonewalling or was she trying to remember?

"Now that we know Josie never got on the plane," Rick added, "every piece of information is more important than ever. Adler came to your house specifically to see Josie. That's not a coincidence."

"Katherine?" Quentin spoke quietly to his wife. "Whatever you know, you must tell."

"I'm just trying to remember something that might help, but I can't think of anything I haven't already told you about that young man. I wish I knew more. Sylvia dead and now Josie and your FBI agent missing. I'm afraid we've opened Pandora's Box and it's going to destroy us all."

Julia had never heard a more apt description for Sylvia Cole's murder and the aftermath than Pandora's Box. Every way she and Rick turned, they uncovered a terrible twist.

And look at Chief McCabe and Laney. Two suspects arrested that Julia knew of so far – the Bradshaw boy and the perverted teacher - and neither of them guilty. She could imagine how defeated they must be feeling, how they must cringe every time the case took another sharp turn.

"Katherine, thank you for calling me about Josie. We'll take all this information straight to Chief McCabe."

"Wait." Quentin stood abruptly and crossed the room to lean against the mantle. "I'm going to put up a million dollar reward for information leading to Josie."

"That should help." Julia said. "You're very generous."

"I can't take any credit." Quentin got that haunted look Julia had seen when he first opened the door. "If it will help find Sylvia's killer, I'll add a million dollars to Zion's reward, too."

"We'll pass that information along to McCabe," Rick said.

"No. I'm going with you."

"If you go, so do I." Katherine's bare feet padded on the polished floor as she came over and laced her arms through her husband's.

He patted her hand. "You don't have to do this. It's my problem."

"Your problem is also mine. I'm going and you might as well not say another word about it."

What was happening here? The tension in the room had just gone up a dozen notches.

"Julia, Agent Richardson...there's one more thing I have to tell you before we go."

As Quentin started talking, Julia imagined his sordid secret spilling out of Pandora's Box and tainting the entire town. One of their most prominent citizens was admitting to producing soft porn and submitting to blackmail.

His tumble from grace would impact the entire town. Not only that, but if Quentin insisted on going public with everything, Sylvia Cole's image as the angel of mercy and the city's brightest young entrepreneur would be tarnished beyond redemption.

Katherine held her husband's hand during his entire confession. It was an amazing show of loyalty, particularly considering Quentin had once exploited women for profit. If his remorse had not been complete and genuine, would she have stood by him? Even though he expressed deep regret, he and Katherine would both be front-page news the moment he went public. The issue of female exploitation was sweeping the country. In some cases, even an accusation without any proof of guilt was enough to destroy a man.

Quentin Windermere was a big target. Isolated by his wealth and years of living a clean, upright life in America's perfect town, he probably didn't grasp the far-reaching consequences of revealing his past in soft porn. He'd be the headline in every major newspaper and television network in America.

He finished his confession with, "This nightmare ends now. Katherine and I will follow you to the station and I'll personally tell McCabe everything."

It was a somber foursome that finally drove away from the Windermere mansion. Julia was surprised to walk outside into fading light and growing shadows.

Her thoughts whirled in a dozen different directions as she turned on her lights and drove toward the Shutter Lake Police Department. She could see Quentin's headlights in her rearview mirror, and she wondered again if he had any idea how his life was about to change.

"Were they telling the truth, Julia?"

She could feel Rick's gaze on her, but she didn't turn his way. Even in the semi-darkness he'd ferret out her conflict.

"Yes. Both of them. About everything."

"What a shame. I like him. Once word gets out, he'll be destroyed."

"Maybe not."

"How do you figure that?"

"This town has something you don't know about, Rick."

"What would that be?"

"Something that has almost disappeared. Pride and tolerance."

Chapter Fifteen

McCabe was glad to be back in his office. Big social events weren't his thing, particularly when they wasted a whole day. But he'd been obligated to attend the concert. There'd been no getting around it. It was his job to protect the dignitaries. Plus, he and Holt had to make a show of force just to keep the whole town from blowing apart.

Nine days and they hadn't found Sylvia's killer.

The way people were looking over their shoulders at the concert, you'd think whoever killed Sylvia in her isolated house in the dark of night was suddenly going to change his MO and start strangling people in the park in broad daylight.

He tossed his jacket over the back of his swivel chair and sank into it. He could use a nap. If he leaned back and shut his eyes for just two minutes it might help.

Holt stuck her head around his doorframe. "Hip still bothering you?"

"I didn't hear that."

She made a face. "Trask is going to get barbecue for supper. You want some?"

"Yeah. And two beers."

"I didn't hear that," she said.

"Smart mouth."

She vanished and he briefly considered putting his feet on his desk and closing his eyes. Two minutes. That's all he asked.

He'd just got one leg up when Trask appeared in his doorway. McCabe banged his boot to the floor. "I thought you were going to Johnny's for barbecue."

"Do you want mild or hot?"

"What the hell? You know I like it hot."

Trask trotted off grinning. Were he and Holt in on this together? Had they made a pact to worry the devil out of him so he'd stay awake and on task? And sober. Don't forget that. He wouldn't put it past either one of them.

He left his comfortable chair, groaning when his weight landed on that bum hip. No drinking for him tonight. Maybe he'd even give it up. See how Holt and Trask would deal with that. He'd been near the top of his class at the police academy. If he sobered up and put his mind to it, he might show them a thing or two about catching a killer.

There had to be something about Sylvia Cole's case that he and Holt were missing. He walked to the filing cabinet and pulled her files. When he sat back down, his hip eased somewhat, and he breathed a sigh of relief.

Give him a day or two – and maybe a good soak with Epsom salts – and he'd be good as new. He flipped open Sylvia's file and started reading.

"Chief?" Officer Lott Delaney was at the door. Now what? McCabe guessed he might as well put a sign outside his office that said Grand Central Station.

"What is it, Delaney?"

"I just got a call from the crime scene at Olive Tree Lane. Somebody took the cupcakes."

"If I've got officers eating the evidence, heads are going to roll."

"No sir. Nobody at SLPD took them."

"Who else would want them? You can't fence cupcakes."

"No, sir. And there's something else."

What now? His corpse had decided to take a stroll down Main Street? "Spit it out, Delaney."

"We've had thirty-six calls come in this afternoon since Zion Cole raised his reward."

Well, hell! Didn't that fool know the more money he offered the more crackpots he'd bring out of the woodwork?

"Did any of them seem legit?"

Delaney walked into his office holding a sheet of paper as long as McCabe's leg. "One from a woman living on Old Mine Road who said she heard Sylvia screaming a man's name the night she was murdered."

"What's she got? X-ray ears? She's all the way over on the south side of town."

"Yes, sir."

"I don't suppose she told you the man's name?"

"She said she didn't hear that part very well."

"You don't say?" Griff picked up his pencil with such force he nearly snapped it in half. "I said *legit.*"

"I thought she might have been driving by Sylvia's house that night. Or next door visiting with a friend."

"Did she tell you that, Delaney?"

"No, sir."

Delaney was young, a rookie cop who'd never been called on to do more than write a traffic ticket in Shutter Lake. Griff was ashamed of himself for taking out his frustration on the kid. Delaney was doing the best he could. They all were.

It was this case. Sylvia's murder was changing all of them. Even Griff. He loved his town and prided himself on running it with an even hand and an even temper. Like his dad before him. Steve McCabe always said courtesy was the hallmark of a gentleman. That had been part of his legacy to the town: he'd been unfailingly courteous as he upheld the law.

"Maybe she was driving by Sylvia's house and just forgot to tell you, Delaney. Keep up the good work. We need every small detail in order to find our killer."

"Yes, sir."

Griff turned back to Sylvia's files and read through the interviews with Wade Travis and Nolan Ikard. He even read through Vinn Bradshaw's. Though the kid was apparently pure as the driven snow and all the evidence had proved his innocence, maybe he'd said something that would open a new line of inquiry. He'd apparently spent lots of time with Sylvia working on a school project.

Nothing jumped out at Griff. What was he missing? He got up and popped a coffee pod into the coffee maker on the table beneath his window. His stomach was rumbling. Maybe the coffee would settle it down.

He glanced out the window and spotted Seth Trask coming up the sidewalk with bags from Johnny's down the street. Great. Griff didn't care for all that exotic food on the square. He'd hardly eaten a thing since breakfast. A good hot meal might put him in the frame of mind to crack this case wide open.

He was picturing his first bite of wet barbecue when Julia Ford's car pulled into the police station's parking lot. The FBI bailed first and then that long stemmed nosey reporter.

What the hell? Was she here to expose his secret? Or was she here to rub his nose in his failure to even come up with a viable suspect in Sylvia Cole's murder?

Another car drove in, one he recognized as belonging to Quentin Windermere. Quentin and Katherine got out and caught up with Julia and the FBI. They had a brief, earnest conversation in the parking lot, and then all four of them headed toward the front door.

For an insane moment Griff considered leaving by the back door. He'd get in his Bronco and go home where he'd saddle Trigger and ride off where nobody could find him. Not even Holt, who was so good at locating him she was bound to be part bloodhound.

Instead he smoothed down his hair, grabbed his coffee cup and headed toward the front to see what fresh hell had caused Julia Ford and one of Shutter Lake's wealthiest, most powerful couples to come calling. Whatever it was, he damned sure wanted Holt to be part of it.

He passed Trask on the way. The smells coming from the bags made Griff's mouth water.

"Just put mine on my desk. Leave Holt's there, too." He and Holt would talk after their unexpected guests left.

Griff rounded the corner and tried not to let his shock show. Quentin Windermere looked like hell, and his wife looked like she'd been crying.

He stuck out his hand. "Mr. Windermere, Mrs. Windermere, what can I do for you?"

Both Windermeres glanced toward Ford as if she were a life raft and they were on the sinking Titanic.

"Chief, we need to talk in private." Ford pinned him with a piercing look. "And I'd like Laney there, too, please."

Hell, Ford didn't sound like she meant *please*. She sounded like she was giving orders.

Griff told Delaney to fetch Holt and a pot of coffee to the conference room, on the double. Then he led the foursome down the hall and pulled out a chair for Katherine Windermere. The woman looked close to collapse.

Only after she was seated did he turn to face the FBI. Ford introduced the man as Special Agent Patrick Richardson.

"Call me Rick." The man's handshake was firm, his eyes steady, his face unreadable. Damn. Richardson was good.

If this was going to be some kind of pissing contest, McCabe and Richardson were an even match. With Griff's bum hip and his supper getting cold on his desk, maybe Richardson had the edge.

Griff slid into his chair just as Holt entered carrying a tape recorder. "Chief, Julia called me moments ago. She has some things to tell us that are pertinent to our case."

His gut tightened. Was the reporter on a witch hunt? Was this the moment when she built the fire under his feet and lit the match?

"What things?"

"She has all the facts. I'll let her tell you."

Julia leaned toward him, her eyes very wide and very blue. Damned. It was like she was seeing right through him.

"Chief McCabe, I know how busy you and Laney are. I'll be brief but thorough. Everything I say will be fact. Nothing will be supposition."

Holt nodded and turned on the tape recorder.

First Julia Ford stated the date, her name and the name of her FBI friend, and then made a simple statement about how they'd uncovered the facts she was about to tell. They'd joined forces on October eleventh to search for two friends, Josie Rodriguez and Special Agent Evan Adler.

The investigative reporter then proceeded to blow McCabe's socks off by naming Josie Rodriguez as a missing person and presenting a time-line that intersected with the subsequent disappearance of FBI Agent Evan Adler and the recent murder of Sylvia Cole.

"Eye witness accounts show Adler trying to connect with Josie and put Sylvia with Adler on multiple occasions in a confined space in time." Julia named her witnesses: Ray Jones, Shonda Reed, Katherine Windermere. "And there's more." She cited Dana Perkins as a witness who had been told of videos of a woman she believed to be Josie on a now-defunct porn site, Viva Venezuela."

McCabe murder case just got a whole lot more complicated.

"Agent Richardson and I are continuing to look into the disappearances of our two friends, and we'll come straight to you with any hard evidence we find."

"Fair enough." McCabe felt an unexpected flash of admiration. He could finally see how a woman as smart and sensible as Laney Holt would be hanging out with Julia Ford.

"Everything else is off the record," Ford said.

McCabe nodded and Holt switched off the recorder.

"Chief McCabe…" Julia turned to her friend and gave a small nod, "Laney, before Mr. Windermere speaks I want to tell you that I've been investigating the Windermeres for quite some time." Katherine gasped and Quentin nodded his approval. "They are two of the finest people I know, sincere in their desire to improve the quality of life in Shutter Lake and devoted to helping exchange students have a better future. I hope you can make it possible for them to continue their wonderful work in peace."

McCabe's relief that Julia had not come to expose him was palpable. He felt positively magnanimous as he nodded.

"Let's hear what he has to say first."

Julia reached over and squeezed Quentin's hand. "I believe in you. You can do this."

The mathematical genius who helped create the Onion Router for browsing the Dark Web stood up to speak. As the words tumbled from his mouth, it was not a genius McCabe saw but a remorseful man unburdening his soul.

~

Later, when their guests were gone, Holt kicked back in her chair in McCabe's office and dug into her bag of cold barbecue. "Damned, Windermere nearly made me cry."

McCabe wasn't about to admit that he'd had to clear his throat one time too many while the dignified man unexpectedly confessed a dirty past. As if that weren't bombshell enough, he'd told how Sylvia had unearthed his secret while cleaning his house and was blackmailing him.

"At least now we have a credible witness who can explain why Sylvia had a pile of cash at her house." Griff pulled out a sandwich and took a big bite. It was cold but that didn't detract from the mouth-watering taste. Johnny's made the best barbecue in California.

"We won't have to use him, McCabe. She was blackmailing the dirt bag, too. Wade Travis."

"You want to keep Windermere lily pure?"

"The man is sixty-six. He's an institution in this town and one of its most generous, civic-minded citizens. He has more than made up for what he did. If we bring him down, the whole town suffers. You tell me, McCabe."

"What about Viva Venezuela?"

"Windermere had nothing to do with that. His porn past was so long ago, I'd be surprised if anybody had one of his films. Or could even remember him in connection with that trade. Besides, he had nothing to do with Josie's disappearance."

"He was the last person to interact with her before she disappeared."

Holt tagged Windermere as innocent with a wave of her hand. "How about that whole airport full of people? What are you trying to do? Play devil's advocate?"

"I'm trying to make heads or tails of a case that's driving us both crazy."

"Speak for yourself, Chief. I'm just here having supper." She took another bite of cold barbecue and winked at him.

"You've got barbecue sauce on your mouth."

"Yeah? How nice of you to notice." She wiped her mouth then wadded her bag and tossed it into the garbage can. "I don't know about you, but I'm ready to blow this joint."

"Holt, that's the smartest thing you've said all day."

Maybe if they got home at a decent hour and got some rest, they might have a brain cell left to come up with a suspect.

Chapter Sixteen

"Dinner," Rick said.

It was an invitation, not a question. But Julia saw no reason to turn it down.

The day had been brutal and exhausting. She couldn't bear the thought of going back to her cottage and having soup from a can again. She usually went to the farmer's market on Saturdays and spent an hour just strolling through the booths. Fresh fruits and vegetable plucked from the fields with the dew still on. Cut flowers and jars of homemade pickles and strawberry jam. Occasionally she found a real treasure, the hand-made quilt she'd hung on a quilt stand at the end of her bed, the hand-carved mug tree she used in the kitchen to hang her favorite mugs.

"Sounds good." She pulled out of the police station's parking lot and headed toward the Wine and Cheese House.

To give Rick credit, he didn't ask where they were going. That's one of things she'd always liked about him, about them together. They were both easy about the little things, where to have dinner, what to do on a leisurely Sunday morning when the rain fell against the window and the planned outing on the lake didn't make sense.

Don't go there, Julia.

She tamped down her memories and told Rick about their destination, that it was a favorite of her girls' night out group and the ambience lent itself to quiet conversation instead of boisterous partying.

"Perfect," he said. "We have lots to talk about."

The Wine and Cheese House was already packed with the Saturday night crowd. Julia requested a booth near the back and was told the wait would be about thirty minutes. She didn't mind. In fact, she treasured the time to lean against the wall and process Quentin Windermere's shocking revelation.

Laney had been sympathetic. Julia could see it in her eyes, her body posture. Even Griff McCabe had seemed more inclined to protect the Windermeres than to drag them through the mud.

And why wouldn't he? If every person's past had to be hung

around his neck like Hawthorne's scarlet letter, there would be a crisis of confidence unlike anything America had ever seen.

"Ready, Julia?" Rick said.

The waitress was waiting for her, smiling. She was new in town. Or maybe she'd been here a while and had never worked the shift when Julia and the girls were here.

Julia followed her through the crowded tables and heard someone call her name. She looked up to see Clifton Trask smiling and waving.

"Who was that?" Rick said when they slid into their booth.

"My dentist."

"It figures. That toothy smile. He was flirting, too."

"He was not. He was reminding me that I'm overdue for my dental checkup and that if I don't get down there soon I'm liable to become a candidate for dentures."

"All that from one little wave?" Julia shot him the bird. "What's his name?"

"Clinton Trask."

"Any relation to Officer Trask?"

Julia should have known Rick wouldn't have missed a single detail at the police station.

"They're brothers." She popped open her menu. Rick ordered an appetizer of stuffed mushrooms and they both ordered corned beef on rye.

"Are the mushrooms still your favorite?"

"Yes." She wasn't about to get into this discussion. "Let's not talk about the past."

"It's the elephant in the room with us. If we don't acknowledge it, we're liable to get crushed."

"Speak for yourself, Rick. I dealt with it a long time ago. I've moved on."

"I haven't and I can't. Not without you. I want you back."

"What does your wife think about that?"

"My divorce is almost final."

"Almost is not good enough."

The food arrived, and Julia was glad for the interruption. In spite of her assurances to Dana, there was a difference between declaring she'd never go back to Rick to her friends and saying it to his face. Rick, in the flesh, was far more seductive than Rick in the abstract.

Finally, he said, "I won't pressure you."

"I won't give you the chance."

"I'm not going to leave Shutter Lake until I know what happened to Adler."

"I know that."

"You're saying you won't help me?"

"No. I'll continue to help you, just as I promised. But I won't be available to you emotionally, Rick. I'm telling you the door to our past is closed."

"I won't accept that. Nothing is ever black and white. Circumstances change, people change. You know that better than most. You've always had an open mind."

"I still do. But I also have a newfound resolve. I'm not picking up where we left off."

"We could start over. After my divorce is final."

"My answer is no."

"Julia…"

Her cell phone rang, cutting off whatever new argument Rick had in mind.

She looked at the screen and was surprised to see the name. *Brenda Lockhart,* she mouthed.

"I dug your number out of my files." Brenda got right to the point. Much like Julia's mother. "I've got to see you and Rick."

Julia glanced at her watch. "Can it wait 'til morning? We're having dinner at the Wine and Cheese House and I don't want to keep you up late."

"I'll wait up. I'm so old I might die in my sleep, and I just remembered something I think you ought to know."

"We'll be right there."

~

Brenda Lockhart waited for them in the reception room at the B&B on Main. She wore a chenille robe and house slippers, and she'd stuffed her hair under a net that barely contained it. The whole conglomeration puffed out from her head like a cumulous cloud.

With her face devoid of makeup, she was barely recognizable. It turned out Brenda drew her eyebrows on. Without them she looked as if she'd been startled by Martians asking for lodging.

"Thank God, you're here." Only the many diamond rings on hands she held out to them tagged her as the flamboyant owner of the B&B. "Sit down. I'm too tired to move and I don't intend to crane my neck while I talk."

They sat on deep cushioned chairs facing her and she started prattling about today's concert on the town square. Had she already forgotten why she'd called? Or was this a wild goose chase, the case of an aging lonely woman who woke up scared and just wanted some company?

"You said you'd remembered something." Julia prodded her.

"Oh, yes. I did. About that car."

This was going to take longer than Julia had thought. Apparently she and Rick were going to have to pull every bit of information from Brenda.

Rick leaned toward her, his face kind. "What car, Mrs. Lockhart?"

"That black one we talked about."

Julia shot Rick an oh-help look. He's the one who'd talked to Brenda about Adler.

"Agent Adler's car?" he said. "A black Jeep Grand Cherokee?"

"That's the one. I saw it."

"Where?"

"Well, it might have been a Grand Cherokee but it might not." Julia thought she might pop out of her skin. "It was dark. I can't count on my foreman to exercise my horses properly, and sometimes when I go back to the ranch at night, I'll take one of the horses out for exercise. I know those trails on my ranch like the back of my hand."

Julia's hopes fell. Here was an unreliable witness who thought she saw something in the dark.

"Take your time, Mrs. Lockhart."

"Brenda…"

"All right, Brenda." Rick displayed the endless patience she'd seen back in Chicago, the capacity to remain unruffled as long as it took for an uncertain witness to get his story straight. "It's understandable if you can't identify the make of the car. Just take your time and tell me exactly what you saw."

"It was a big black car. I know that much."

"And why do think it might be Adler's car?"

"Well, you said he was driving a black car and there was one person in it. A man."

"Could you tell anything about him? His size? What he was wearing?"

"No. It was too dark. A little bit overcast. You know, one of those nights when the moon slips in and out of the clouds and there aren't many stars."

"I do," he said. "You're doing fine."

"Mill River runs behind my property and connects it with that old mine out there on the south side of town. The trail I like best takes me right by the river bridge. Occasionally I'll see kids parked down there. Necking, I guess, or whatever they call it nowadays."

"What was the man doing?" Rick said.

"I thought it was unusual, just one man on the bridge all by himself late at night. That's why it stuck with me.'"

Rick shot Julia a look that telegraphed his growing frustration. She took over. "Brenda, I have a few questions. If you can give me specific answers the way you did in the interview – remember?" Brenda nodded. "Then Rick and I will leave so you can go back to bed. I don't want to keep you up too late."

Brenda chuckled. "You're something else, Julia Ford." She straightened the hair net that had slid sideways and threatened to cover her left eye. "Fire away. I'll behave now."

"What was the man doing?" Julia decided to give Brenda multiple-choices. "Sitting in his car? Walking nearby? Standing on the bridge?"

"He was standing at the railing, just looking at the water."

"Could you tell what he was looking at? A boat in the river? A big log? Anything unusual?"

"No. But there was something about him that gave me the shivers. I stopped my horse and watched him."

"For how long? A few minutes? An hour?"

"About five minutes, I'd say. That's a long time to stare at nothing."

"I agree. What did the man do next?"

"He got in his car and drove off, and I rode my horse back to the stables."

The facts were lining up for Julia and she didn't like the picture they painted. A dark night, a black car, a deep river. One person dead and two missing.

"Brenda, do you remember the date?"

"I don't remember dates unless they're written down. Never could. The thing that makes this incident stick in my mind is that a few weeks later, Sylvia Cole was murdered."

Chapter Seventeen

Sunday, October 14

Julia didn't need anything to wake her. The sun, an alarm clock, even her own circadian rhythm. Brenda's previous night's revelation prodded her from the bed at sunrise. She showered and dressed quickly, jeans, top of the line track shoes. Much better for running than high heels. She added a heavy sweater to ward off the early morning chill. When the sun started climbing, she could tie it around her waist.

Without opening curtains, she hurried to her kitchen to nab coffee and a granola bar. On second thought she grabbed an extra bar for Rick. They'd eat in the car. Mill River bordered miles of Brenda Lockhart's ranch. Their search would start at the river bridge, but it could take them far beyond. And all day. They wanted to utilize every minute of daylight.

She pushed open her front door. Clouds. A threatening sky. Rain was the last thing they needed today.

Julia backtracked and grabbed a hooded raincoat from her hall closet. She spotted a slicker Joe had bought the last time he and Rachel visited, and nabbed it off the hanger. While she was at it, she might as well take the oversized umbrella too…and some extra food in case they had to stay at the river all day.

She was turning into her mother. Rachel had taught her the value of always being prepared. It was a lesson that had worked well…until Julia forgot. Until she unknowingly went to meet a serial killer with nothing but a cell phone, a pair of stiletto pumps and a big attitude.

Julia shook off the memory, surprised that it didn't send shivers, surprised it didn't cause the least sign of a panic attack. Could it be that old wound was finally closing?

She stowed her supplies into the back seat and drove to the B&B on Main. Rick was waiting for her on the front porch.

She parked in front and when he climbed in, she tossed him a granola bar.

"Thanks. This might come in handy later."

"You've already had breakfast?" She pulled away from the curb and took the turn that would take her to Old Mine Road.

"One big enough for the proverbial log rolling. Ham and biscuits. Brenda didn't want me to go hungry during the search."

"You could have tucked a ham and biscuit in your pocket for me."

"You never did like ham and biscuits, Julia. Even when your mother made them. What's up with the attitude?"

"This case. The search." Just beyond the outskirts of town, raindrops spattered her windshield. "The rain."

He didn't say anything for a while, just studied her then glanced in the back seat and assessed her raincoat, the slicker, the umbrella, the cooler. She'd even brought along some magazines on antiques in case they had some down time. He didn't comment. He didn't speculate that since her unintentional stay with a killer her desire for preparedness might be bordering on obsession.

Nor did he indicate that he was going to try to change her mind about resurrecting their relationship. Good. Hopefully that meant he'd accepted her no as final.

Once they got out of the city limits they saw the real beauty of the valley. The Sierras rose in sharp relief against a sky that was still high and wide and spectacular in spite of the rain. The sharp bare peaks gave way to a thick slope of trees, evergreens that gave the valley the feel of abundant life and deciduous trees wearing their fall coats of gold and red.

They passed a few houses, smaller and far less showy than the ones in Shutter Lake, interspersed among a scattering of small truck farms. Old Mine Road was lined with fields of late food crops that still supplied the farmer's market.

A long stretch with thinning trees and open meadows gave way to Brenda Lockhart's ranch. She hadn't given it a name nor put a fancy sign to announce she had property on both sides of the road. But her well-kept fences and her horses showing their thoroughbred lineage announced loud and clear that Rick and Julia were entering a little slice of bluegrass Kentucky transported to the Sierras.

"Impressive," he said. "Peaceful. I could retire here."

Julia suspected that was meant for her, but she let the remark slide. She made the turn onto a less traveled road that would take them to the bridge over Mill River. Thankfully the rain had slowed to a steady drizzle.

The woods had grown thicker here, and some of the trees were so tall they made a natural canopy over the road. No wonder the town's young lovers sought out the bridge for their secret liaisons.

"Bridge's coming up." Rick's voice was the only thing about him that showed his tension. Was he still haunted by Shonda's question? Had he had second thoughts about the possibility that Evan Adler killed Sylvia and then vanished? Or perhaps killed one woman – Josie Rodriguez - then went looking for another?

Julia turned into a natural clearing where the packed earth and flattened leaves showed where others had parked there many times. They got out and headed toward the bridge without raingear. It would hamper their movements and they'd prefer a drizzle to the hassle. Julia hoped the rains held off.

The bridge was old and built with enormous trestles that could hold up the mining trucks with their heavy loads. The ancient railing that ran along both sides was only waist high. If you wanted to jump into the river, you'd have to climb over. But if you wanted to throw something into the water, even something as heavy as a body, it wouldn't take much effort to lift it up a few feet and then toss. Especially if you were a man whose profession required you stay physically fit.

They stood on the bridge looking at the dark, swirling water. Julia had always thought Mill River looked forbidding at this spot. Something to do with the water's depth and the shadow of trees.

It was even more so today, with the rain and the knowledge of what Brenda had seen.

"How far away do you think Brenda was?"

Rick was good at that. Reading her mind.

Julia scanned the forest beyond the fences that bordered the river. When she'd done the long-ago interview, Brenda had taken her on the back trails.

"There." She pointed to a small break among the trees. Even in the mists you could see a faint trail winding through the woods.

"Close enough to get a good look at the car," he said.

"Yes. Even in the dark."

They searched the water a while, but it gave up no secrets.

"Let's go down," she said.

"Together or separate?"

"I know this area. For now, stick with me."

A shiver ran along her spine. Maybe her request was self-serving. Maybe she didn't want to be alone with whatever they found. Or maybe she was afraid the man in the black car might be somewhere in those deep woods watching.

"You okay, Julia? I can do this by myself."

"I'm fine." She plowed ahead. The embankment down to the river was steep and the rains had made it slick. Her feet slid and she caught a sapling to stop her headlong plunge into the river.

She slowed her pace and kept a careful watch where she was stepping. By the time they got to the edge of the water, the rains had started in earnest again. Within minutes it had soaked through her sweater.

"Some big planner I am."

"I can go back and get the raincoats."

"No. It'll waste too much time."

She picked up a long, sturdy stick that would serve as both hiking stick and probe into the thick undergrowth. Rick did the same thing.

"I'll go ahead and search back in this direction," he said.

She nodded. They'd cover twice as much ground that way.

As he plunged ahead Julia began a methodical search along the riverbanks underneath the bridge. The rain stopped abruptly and the sun shot feeble beams through the tree canopy. She shed her wet sweater and tossed it over a bush that would either help it dry or tear it to shreds.

Her stomach rumbled as she went back to her search. It must be around lunchtime and her granola bar wasn't holding up. Why hadn't she tucked another one into her pocket? Next time she did this she'd bring a fanny pack.

If there was a next time.

Suddenly her probe hit something solid in the bushes. With her heart slamming, Julia bent down and parted the leaves only to discover a rotting hamper somebody had abandoned on a long-ago picnic.

Rick was no longer in sight, but she could hear his search, the thud of his stick against river rocks and the crunch of the debris under his shoes.

The sun dried Julia's hair and made her wish she'd at least brought a bottle of water down the embankment.

"Got something!" Rick yelled.

She headed in the direction of his voice. He wouldn't move whatever he'd found. He'd leave the scene as he'd found i.

She could see him now, kneeling on the ground.

"What is it?" she called.

"A running shoe. Fairly new."

Who walked off and left behind a practically new shoe?

Nobody.

Julia picked up speed, moving as fast as the undergrowth would let her. She hadn't even broken a sweat when she knelt beside Rick. The generic white leather shoe with green and blue stripes could have belonged to either gender. Except for the size.

Her heart clinched.

"It's a woman's shoe," she said. "And a small woman at that."

It appeared to be intact, but leather would last for years without decomposing. The slight fading of colors and the collection of mud and debris indicated the shoe had been beside the river more than a day or two.

Was it possible the shoe had been there two and half months? Since Josie was last seen?

"Did you see anything else?" The sight of that lone shoe made her so sorrowful she whispered.

"No. Did you?"

She shook her head and studied the shoe. It told a story she could feel in her bones, a story she couldn't unravel by herself.

Rick put his hand over hers. "You can call McCabe and your friend Laney."

She was grateful he understood. Shutter Lake was her town and the girl missing one shoe was her responsibility. At least until the team of law enforcement could arrive and start dragging the river.

~

The lone shoe unleashed a frenzy, even in nature. By the time McCabe and Laney arrived with their team of forensics and divers, with their nets and diving gear, rain was coming down in torrents.

Julia and Dana huddled in raincoats under a big umbrella while

Rick stayed down below doing what he could to help with the search.

"I'm so glad you called me, even if I don't recall ever seeing that particular shoe on Josie."

"I never considered otherwise, Dana."

"You think it's hers, don't you?"

"I don't know."

"But your spidey senses are saying it is, aren't they?"

There was no fooling Dana about anything. Ever. No need to even try.

"Yes."

Sounds drifted up to them, the net being cast and hauled then dragged to the bank empty. Men calling to each other across the water. One question. *Did you find anything?* Only two answers, yes or no, and both of them horrible beyond imagining.

Laney shielded her face against the rain and looked up at them, waved. They waved back then gave her the thumbs up.

"She's being brave," Dana said. "This is killing her. The possibility of finding another young woman dead from violence."

"I know."

"No matter what happens, we're in this together. We've got each other."

"Yes. And Ana." Julia didn't have the heart to tease Dana by calling her Mother Hen or any number of silly nicknames she'd made up at girls' night out.

Teams of two continued their search along the riverbanks while the boat moved farther down river. Divers went once more into the murky, churning waters. Julia's watch showed they had only another two hours before it would be too dark to search.

"I've got cupcakes from Batter Up in the car." Dana had been at the bakeru when Julia called.

"I'm not hungry."

"You've been here all day. Have you eaten anything?"

"Yes." Besides the granola bar she'd had this morning, Julia had choked down half of another one when she and Rick climbed back up the embankments and turned the heater in her vehicle on full blast trying to dry off and get warm.

Suddenly the rain stopped and the sun that had struggled to show its face all day put on a final show of red and purple and gold.

"GOT SOMETHING!"

The call echoed over the water, froze the two on the bridge and the teams searching and waiting on the riverbanks. There was a cathedral-like silence as the diver came out of the water with his burden. The remains of a small body with long dark hair trailing like seaweed. Severe decomposition had rendered the victim barely more than a skeleton, but bits of clothing still clung to the lower body, tatters of denim and one track shoe. White leather with faded green and blue stripes.

Dana smothered a cry and peered through the opera glasses she always kept in her glove compartment. Her lips trembled as she silently passed them to Julia.

In the glow of sunset the bones took on an ethereal glow. The body in the river might have been an angel, returning as a torch of justice.

Julia lowered the small binoculars and watched Laney separate herself from the crowd that suddenly sprang back to life as the remains were brought ashore. The deputy chief stopped briefly to say something to Rick and McCabe, then continued her way up the embankment to the bridge.

"It's her, isn't it?" Dana's voice cracked. "Josie?"

"There's nothing to indicate that yet." Laney's face showed the careful way she was controlling her feelings. "We have severely decomposed remains, probably a young female judging by the hair and the size of the bones. But we won't know the identity until we see a report from the medical examiner."

"How long will it take to get dental records?"

"Dana, hush." Julia grabbed her hand. "Laney's got this."

"You're damned right, I have. Nobody does this to a young girl in my town and gets away with it."

Whatever she'd seen down there – whatever had been done to that haunting dead girl with the mermaid hair – had chipped a piece off her soul. Laney moved under the umbrella, and the three women hovered in a somber circle while another ritual of death played out below them.

They were caught in a net of grief and horror until the latest dead girl was finally covered with a body bag and disappeared from their view. Finally they all came up like swimmers for air and stood a while blinking at each other, trying to comprehend that yet another heinous crime had been committed in their once-perfect paradise.

Julia gripped the handle of her umbrella so hard her knuckles turned white. The chances of that young girl kicking off one shoe, stripping naked to the waist then walking into the water were nil. First Sylvia Cole was found dead and now the girl in the water. Someone was killing young women in this town and he was still out there.

She was unaware that she was shaking until raindrops rolled off the brim of her umbrella and plopped onto Laney's shirt.

"Julia," Laney spoke in her firm way that said she was going to burst out of the awful spell or die trying. "Are you going to put that thing down, or am I going to have to haul you off to jail?"

"For what?"

"Obstruction of sunset."

Given the circumstances, it didn't crack them up but it did coax a smile. And wasn't that what friendship was all about? Helping each other through the hard times as well as the good? Giving each other courage when the instinct is to hunker down and shut out the rest of the world?

"I've got to get back down there." Laney turned and gave them her no-nonsense look. "If word leaks out about this, I'm going to skin some hides."

"Yes, ma'am." Dana gave her a mock salute.

"Julia, get her out of here. Call Ana and grab a table at the Wine and Cheese House. I'm calling an emergency meeting."

"What's on the agenda besides stuffed mushrooms?" Julia already guessed, but in the face of that crime scene below the bridge, she was trying to keep from falling apart. They all were.

"Murder." As usual, Laney didn't pull any punches. "I've got two dead girls and at least one killer on the loose. One who might be getting ready to strike again. I need all the help I can get."

"You're barking up the right tree," Dana said. "There's more brain power in the four of us than in the rest of this town combined."

"I won't tell the school board you said that." Laney strode off, the hint of a smile playing around her lips.

Julia linked arms with Dana. "Come on, Sherlock. You heard what the boss said. We've got to get cracking on this case."

"I'm thinking about making us some Wonder Woman suits."

"Better make them with long pants. Laney's the only one with good legs."

"Speak for yourself, Julia."

The great thing is that Julia had – several times in the last few days. And it felt good. More like the intrepid woman she'd been years ago.

The trick was to remain true to herself, to move forward with courage and resolve – especially when that resolve meant she would continue using her investigative skills to help stop the killer who was still on the loose in Shutter Lake.

Somehow they had to find the truth amid all the lies.

The End

Thank you for reading! If you enjoyed this novel, kindly consider leaving a review on Amazon.

Continue reading to find out what happens next in Shutter Lake!

SNEAK PEEK: WHAT SHE KNEW

Enjoy this Sneak Peek of the final BREAKDOWN

book, *what she knew* by Regan Black

©2018

Chapter One

Sunday October 14

Her house of cards was swaying. About to topple.

Dr. Luciana Perez sat in her home office, her chair turned toward the gray, rainy evening on the other side of the window. The vibrant fall color of the trees behind her house had been muted by the weather as well as her mood. On the desk, her cell phone chimed with yet another text message alert and she ignored it, her courage momentarily failing her.

She'd heard the news via text an hour ago and she had yet to shake off the chill that washed over her. A young woman, stripped to the waist, had been pulled from the river. The body was not immediately recognizable, thanks to the natural course of decomposition, but she could almost hear the name in the ping and patter of raindrops against the glass: *Josie Rodriguez.*

Ana had never been more grateful that her scope of work at the Shutter Lake Medical Clinic didn't include serving as the coroner.

The text message notifying her about the body had been from

her friend Dana Perkins. Dana, a superb psychologist and principal of Shutter Lake School, had been worried about Josie for weeks. Ana knew this wasn't the answer Dana had hoped for when she asked their friend Julia Ford, a former investigative reporter to look into the girl's disappearance.

Maybe it wasn't Josie after all.

If only. A bitter, half-sob slipped through Ana's lips. If the remains turned out to be someone other than Josie, the tension and fear gripping Shutter Lake would only increase exponentially. She had a few patients who didn't need that kind of stress exacerbating underlying concerns and conditions.

Some of the brightest minds in industry, technology, and banking had come together to build and develop this town, planting their idea of paradise in the gorgeous Sierra Mountains of northern California. From the school to the cutting edge medical clinic she ran to the commitment to the arts, Shutter Lake had been a slice of heaven. More than a home, here she'd found the peace and stability she needed to heal even as she engaged her skills to heal others.

She loved being their doctor, caring for the community as a whole. Her staff, carefully selected, had become a second family and a high-functioning team every bit as essential to delivering excellent care as the state-of-the-art equipment the city council provided.

Murder had changed that.

A familiar voice in her head urged her to run. Now, before she became the next victim.

Now. Quickly. Tonight.

But where could she possibly go?

At forty, with years of experience in private practice, her resume should stand on its own. But what if her next employer picked away the thin veneer hiding her past like old polish chipping off a fingernail? The world was becoming smaller every day and previously buried secrets were up for grabs. Sylvia Cole's murder was all the encouragement Ana needed to tread lightly.

This position had been the equivalent of a lightning strike, the right opportunity opening up at the perfect time. The seamless combination of the well-equipped clinic, the stunning house, and the reliable support of a city council focused on encouraging healthy lifestyle choices was so rare as to be almost mythical. She'd been a fool to assume it could last forever.

As Dr. Perez, she'd often been praised for her medical brilliance and compassion with patients, but she'd done herself a great disservice by allowing her escape hatch to rust over. She rested her head against the cool window glass. After everything, it was hard to accept that complacency in the midst of a compassionate effort would be her undoing.

Seeking to calm her skittering nerves, she told herself it was only a problem if she survived the current crisis. Assuming the person who'd murdered Sylvia was also responsible for the disappearances of Josie and a missing FBI agent. If that person managed to kill her next, she wouldn't be in a position to care what skeletons spilled from her closet.

She closed her eyes, well aware that she wasn't ready to give up, give in, or die. Where did that leave her? Alive or dead, she couldn't see a way that this situation ended well for her. That meant it was time to get proactive about either telling the truth or escaping Shutter Lake.

Her phone chimed again, twice. Someone needed her attention, needed her to put her own worries aside. Reminding herself she'd overcome enormous obstacles to reach this respected status in a community that cared for her as much as she cared for it, she rallied and picked up her phone.

Not the clinic. The message had come through in two parts from the deputy chief of police, Laney Holt. She was requesting an emergency girls' night out. The second text specified the Wine and Cheese House and a later than usual time due to the circumstances of finding a body in the river.

Having three girls' nights in one week was unprecedented. Clearly, times had changed in Shutter Lake.

A third message popped up from Julia. She and Dana would get a table and Ana and Laney were expected to arrive as soon as possible. Ana sent a quick confirmation.

Barring an emergency, Ana had no excuse to avoid the gathering. Deep down, the wounded girl she'd been warred with the woman she'd become. This wasn't the time to give in to old fears. Laney, the only member of the Shutter Lake PD with experience investigating murder, had been diligently working to find Sylvia's killer. If she could overcome the trauma that drove her to leave a good career as a detective with the Los Angeles PD, Ana could pull herself together and be supportive.

Here in Shutter Lake, she'd learned that's what friends did. Support, listen, nurture. Friends had been a rare commodity in Ana's life and it still surprised her that she had four—no, three. Sylvia was dead. God, she missed her. Her heart felt sluggish whenever Sylvia came to mind and these days, with a murderer on the loose, it was impossible to think of anything else.

The younger woman had been born and raised here and grown into a vibrant, vital part of the community. And she'd gone out of her way to welcome Ana. They'd bonded over their mutually fierce independence and love of chocolate. In Sylvia, she'd found a confidant she'd never dared to hope for.

Still, to have three women in that treasured category of friendship was a big accomplishment considering where she'd started.

Naturally the discovery of a second body, another young woman, would affect everyone in town as the news spread. Shutter Lake had been shocked when Sylvia, a respected entrepreneur, creator and owner of Sparkle cleaning service, was found murdered in her home. Sylvia's parents were devastated and her father kept upping the reward for any information leading to justice for his daughter.

But Ana's friends would be taking this discovery harder than most in town, for vastly different reasons. All four of them had settled in Shutter Lake, choosing lucrative, lower-stress jobs that allowed them to hide and heal from tragedy-laden pasts.

Laney had found a measure of peace in the slower pace of Shutter Lake after devastating events during the case that was her last with the LAPD. Dana arrived eager to move forward and determined to serve faculty and students here after losing four of her Kindergarten students during a school shooting in Phoenix. Julia still dealt with lingering panic and aftershocks, especially this time of year. While following a story on the Jack o' Lantern serial killer of Chicago, she'd been kidnapped by the monster and only escaped by killing him.

As their primary physician, Ana was privy to how those dreadful events impacted her patients. Having personally escaped a vicious start in life, she knew firsthand how the old memories could crop up and interfere at the most inopportune times.

They all worked daily to stay ahead of the ghosts haunting

them. Having friends to be open with cast a light into the shadows, dispelling those ghosts.

Tell them.

Her breath stuttered in and out of her lungs and she quickly dismissed the thought. There were some things friends couldn't change. Some secrets that, once shared, would only backfire and hurt everyone.

Sylvia's murder was proof enough of that. She'd done more than keep her clients' homes clean. She'd observed and discovered secrets ranging from curious to problematic. As far as Ana knew Sylvia had never once broadcast those secrets. Still, it was likely someone had killed her to keep her quiet. Although Ana had a vague notion about the killer's identity, she didn't have evidence to back up her theory. Laney needed more than speculation to close out this investigation.

Swallowing her anguish over losing a dear friend, Ana deliberately shifted her thinking toward her analytical side. Yolanda Cole, Sylvia's mother was suffering from increasing grief and stress issues. In the days since her daughter's body had been found she'd been to the clinic twice —once for chest pains and once for sleeplessness. Ana made a mental note to ask Laney tonight when the police intended to release Sylvia's body. Yolanda and Zion needed the emotional closure despite the ongoing investigation.

Her lower lip trembled and she caught it between her teeth. Tears blurred her vision much like the rain blurred the view outside her window. She'd cried over Sylvia, privately, and would likely do so again. But not now when swollen, red-rimmed eyes would only bring unwanted attention from her friends. With everything they were dealing with, her personal grief was the least of their trouble.

Any minute now, Ana would be strong enough, clear-eyed enough to drive back into town, passing by Sylvia's house still marred with crime scene tape, to meet her friends.

She took a deep breath. And another. Striding out of her office, she paused in the hall bath and brushed her hair, pulling it back into a sleek ponytail, dabbing a little gloss onto her lips. At the hall tree by the front door, she dropped her phone into her purse and unhooked her keys from the leather tab that held them. Staying organized kept her calm. That calm had carried her through the highs and lows of remaking her life.

Setting her alarm system and activating the cameras inside and out, she headed for her car. Her cell phone hummed with a message just before she turned from her drive to Olive Tree Lane. A little ashamed that she hoped it was an emergency, she braked and grabbed the phone to check.

The text message was from Dana, suggesting she hurry if she wanted any of the stuffed mushrooms. Amused, Ana felt her lips curl and her heart lift. Leave it to Dana to say just the right thing, whether she knew it or not. The woman had a gift and it was a pleasure to coordinate with such a talented professional when a patient needed both of them.

When Ana reached the restaurant, decorated with the seasonal golds and ambers of fall, she was steadier and grateful for it. The three women had a glass of her favorite wine waiting for her as she slid into the booth to join them. Yes, friends were a treasure.

She looked at each of them in turn, soaking up the glow of happiness that she'd found a place to belong. Even if it couldn't last, she wouldn't toss away such a rare joy in the midst of an emotion-ridden crisis. Changing names to protect the innocent didn't make her any less their friend.

"You okay?" Dana asked.

"Great," she lied smoothly.

Julia nudged the plate with one lone stuffed mushroom closer to her. "Long day?"

"Not as long as yours," Ana replied. She was pleased to see they'd all taken the time to change into warm, dry clothing before coming back out tonight. None of them were showing typical cold symptoms, but if she could make it easier on them she would.

She patted her purse. "I stopped by the clinic and picked up some cold medicine samples. It wasn't the best day to be outside for hours on end." Taking care of the physical was only one part of the equation in her mind.

"You can take the doctor out of the clinic," Laney said with a wry chuckle. "Can't take the clinic out of the doc."

"We're all happy to be alive enough to catch a cold," Julia murmured into her wine. "Poor Josie."

Laney shot her a quelling glance. "We don't have an ID on the victim yet."

Though the odds of them being overheard were low, Ana appreciated Laney's caution.

"She'd clearly been in the water a while," Julia said with a small shudder.

"Which makes identification more challenging," Laney reminded her in low tones.

Ana kept her professional mask in place to hide her revulsion at the images that comment evoked. As the primary physician for an entire town, she'd quickly learned to hide any inkling of judgment over anything her patients divulged. Laney had proven equally circumspect with information regarding the investigation.

"Hopefully we'll know something before the press conference tomorrow," Laney continued.

"Usual time?" Julia asked.

"And the usual place," Laney confirmed.

All of the press conferences since Sylvia's death had been held in front of City Hall on Monday evenings at five o'clock. Based on what Ana was seeing with her patients, she wasn't sure the gatherings were reassuring the community as much as the police department and city council hoped.

Laney raised her wine glass to her lips. With her blond hair pulled back into a ponytail, her unframed face appeared far too young for the horrors she'd seen along the way.

"I really wish I could have identified her," Dana murmured, staring into her wine.

Ana exchanged a knowing look with Laney as she patted Dana's shoulder. "The officials will handle it. Soon, I'm sure."

"Laney didn't let me close enough," Dana continued. "I get it," she added, summoning a weak smile for the deputy chief. "I just wanted to spare the Windermeres."

In their sixties, Katherine and Quentin Windermere had been instrumental in founding the town. They'd never had children of their own so they hosted exchange students every semester. Josie Rodriguez had stayed with them for a short time, diving into the community so deeply she even took a part-time job with Sparkle. Then one day, she was simply gone. Katherine had called the school to inform Dana well after the fact, explaining Josie would be absent because she'd returned to Venezuela for a family emergency.

"Her mother's nearby," Julia said to Dana. "And I'm sure there's DNA somewhere between her room at the Windermere's or even Sparkle. Right Laney?"

"You know I can't discuss any details of the investigation," Laney said.

"Right. You also know we're here because *you* asked us to come. Between the four of us we're practically a brain trust," Dana reminded her. "Four heads are better than one and you need a solid lead."

"True," Laney allowed. She looked directly at Ana. "You knew Sylvia better than we did. Any thoughts on who wanted her dead?"

Tell them.

Sylvia had never joined them for girls' night, despite Ana's invitations and encouragement. Respecting that, she shook her head. "No one has confessed," she replied. "Unless you're asking about a specific patient, suspected of criminal behavior, confidentiality is still binding."

Laney only pursed her lips.

"In my professional opinion," Ana continued, "Sylvia was not disposed to violence." Ana rolled her shoulders. "As her friend, I can assure you she never told me she wanted to toss anyone in a river, much less an employee she delighted in. Assuming the remains belong to Josie."

"I'm not attacking you, Ana," Laney said, her voice cool. "Just looking for insight."

Ana supposed between them, she and Dana and Laney knew most of Shutter Lake's secrets. People tended to trust the three of them. If only Sylvia's killer would confide in one of them, by accident or design, they might make some progress.

"I understand." Ana stayed calm as three pairs of eyes studied her. "This is difficult for all of us." She sipped her wine. "What made you go down to the river?" Ana asked Julia.

"Dana," Julia replied. "You know she asked me to dust off my investigative reporting skills and dig into Josie's disappearance."

Ana nodded. Nothing mattered to Dana as much as the safety and welfare of her students.

"So you could focus on Sylvia," Dana said to Laney.

"I was never offended," Laney replied with a warm, confident smile.

It was a lovely expression that nurtured trust and defused tension whether Laney was taking a statement on a missing dog or dealing with a fender bender. Until Sylvia's murder that had been the worst of crimes to cope with in Shutter Lake.

Unfortunately, it was not the expression Laney aimed Ana's way tonight. She couldn't decipher what her friend was thinking, only the unsettling reaction it created. Had the investigation turned up something—past or present—that pointed to Ana as a suspect?

Run.

She wanted to rip that voice out of her head. Fear, panic, or knee-jerk reactions never solved anything.

"Ana?" Julia tapped her fingernail on the table.

She blinked rapidly, clearing away the cobwebs of her past. "Yes, sorry. You were saying?"

"A witness remembered seeing a man standing alone on the Mill River bridge, staring at the water a few weeks back," Julia explained. "She couldn't pin down the exact date and she didn't have much of a description since it was late at night, but like you with the cold meds, we followed intuition and went to look around."

"Are you all right?" Ana's question was for all of them.

"Finding that shoe tangled in the brush didn't leave me much hope for a positive outcome," Julia admitted. "I wanted so badly to be wrong and have you three accuse me of turning back into a cynical reporter."

The laughter around the table was brittle and brief.

"I can't imagine the shock of it," Ana said. Except she could, having faced the grim finality of death before her twelfth birthday, long before her studies in medical school.

Julia twisted her wineglass side to side, watching the golden liquid roll and glide. "Now we just need to find Special Agent Adler."

"The hunk's missing partner?" she asked, trying to make Julia smile.

It almost worked. Julia's old flame, Special Agent Patrick Richards had come to town less than a week ago on the trail of his partner Evan Adler who seemed to have disappeared. Julia had adamantly sworn off rekindling any romance with Rick but Ana recognized the telltale signs of Julia struggling with old memories. The fall season troubled her enough without having her ex around.

When asked, she'd told Julia she hadn't seen Adler. It wasn't a lie, but it wasn't the full truth either. Sylvia had mentioned the FBI agent was coming to town to visit with her about Josie's disappearance. Ana's stomach twisted. Recognizing the signs of anxiety, she once again coached herself away from the abyss of full disclosure.

If she blurted out everything right now, she wouldn't be able to help people who needed her still. Patients like Yolanda, wrecked by grief, and Troy Duval who was dealing with the progression of his Multiple Sclerosis.

Better to wait for the facts to come in. If the girl from the river wasn't Josie, Ana would have exposed herself to persecution—and worse—for no reason.

"If the girl you found is Josie, why would the Windermeres cover up her disappearance?" Ana queried.

"They didn't know," Julia said. "They believed the family emergency thing. Quentin saw her through security. Then poof." She flicked her fingers.

Ana had her doubts. She met Laney's gaze. "What about her family?"

"Her parents came up to Grass Valley when she got the exchange student spot," Laney said. "After so much time without any word, they'd gone to the local police to list her as missing."

"Naturally, they haven't looked too hard," Julia muttered. "Lumping her in with the typical angst-ridden teenagers who turn into runaways. Her mother recently met with Mr. and Mrs. Windermere too, begging for help to find her."

Josie hadn't been typical. She'd been responsible, smart, and determined to make a better life by following Sylvia's example. "Venezuela isn't exactly known for reliable infrastructure." Ana's mind was spinning. "If her parents were here, so close..." She looked to Dana.

The school principal brushed at the red fringe of her bangs. "Josie would've lost her position at our school if we'd found out her parents lived nearby. I can't blame her and the Windermeres for hiding that fact and I commend her for finding a job to help out her parents."

"Sylvia thought the world of Josie." At Laney's sharp glance Ana wished she could reel the words back in. "They cleaned the clinic together a couple of times." Ana traced the curve of her wine glass, wondering how best to proceed. Jumping the gun could cost her, yes, but it could also be a detriment to the investigation if she sent Laney down the wrong path.

This town needed answers about the crisis, not more drama from the doctor they counted on to be calm and collected. When no one else seemed eager to continue the discussion about Josie or

Sylvia, Ana steered the conversation in a less volatile direction, grateful when Dana picked up the cues with talk of the upcoming Fall Carnival for the school. Dana even managed to wrangle a few volunteer hours out of each of them for the event.

"I'm going by Batter Up tomorrow," Dana said. "Hopefully Heidi is willing to donate a cake for the cake walk booth and," she crossed her fingers, "cupcakes for the bake sale table."

"Better you than me," Julia said. "The woman can hardly be civil to me."

"I need to speak with her as well," Laney said. "Let me know when you're done."

"What did she do, shoplift butter?" Julia joked.

Ana hoped not. At her last physical, Heidi's bad cholesterol levels were on the high end.

Laney gave them her *I'm-not-at-liberty-to-say* look. "Nothing like that. Considering how prickly she's been lately, I don't want her turning down Dana because I put her in a bad mood."

"She's either prickly or chattering like a hen." Julia flicked her fingers. "There's a reason I prefer The Grind. Nolan and his staff are steady."

"The investigation has everyone on edge," Ana said. Her hours meant she didn't get to the bakery often, thank goodness. One taste of Heidi's chocolate delight frosting and she'd been hooked. Well aware of her weakness for decadent sweets, Ana typically saved Batter Up treats for the quarterly birthday parties at the clinic.

The rain had finally moved out of the area by the time the four of them settled the check and headed to the parking lot to go their separate ways. Ana stopped Laney before she could move toward her vehicle. "I didn't want to ask in front of the others. When do you think the Coles can claim Sylvia's body?"

She couldn't breach confidentiality and tell Laney outright that it would help Yolanda, but it was a no-brainer that a mother would want to lay her only child to rest.

"I'm sure it will be soon. The report was filed and evidence collected. I'll call the coroner first thing in the morning and lean a little."

"Thank you, Laney."

At her car, Ana slid behind the wheel and just sat there for a minute. Staring out into the darkness, the streets gleaming after the rain, she knew what she had to do. Once her contingency plan was in order, she would write out everything for Laney. What she knew, what she suspected, and how it might tie everything together.

Then she'd leave before Laney was forced to lock her up. It wasn't ideal, deceiving her friends, but it was her only hope to stay ahead of the nightmares she'd been running from for the past twenty-six years.

DON'T MISS

…a single book of the stunning BREAKDOWN series!
Debra Webb, the dead girl *(Breakdown,* Book 1)

Vicki Hinze, so many secrets *(Breakdown,* Book 2)

Peggy Webb, all the lies *(Breakdown,* Book 3)

Regan Black, what she knew *(Breakdown,* Book 4)

…. the Short Read Prequels

In the BREAKDOWN novels, Laney, Dana, Julia and Ana are haunted by their pasts. Find out why in the prequels. Get all four. For details, visit the authors' websites.

Debra Webb, *no looking back,* www.debrawebb.com (Laney's story)
Vicki Hinze, *her deepest fear,* www.vickihinze.com (Dana's story)
Peggy Webb, *just one look,* www.peggywebb.com (Julia's story)
Regan Black, *trust no one,* www.reganblack.com (Ana's story)

ABOUT THE AUTHOR

Peggy Webb is an actress, musician and award-winning author. The former adjunct instructor at Mississippi State University lives in the Deep South among the gardens she designed and planted. Peggy has written more than 80 novels in multiple genres, including literary fiction as **Elaine Hussey**. Pat Conroy called her work "astonishing" and reviewers hail her as "one of the Southern literary greats." Visit her and sign up for her newsletter at www.peggywebb.com. Follow her on Facebook, Twitter and Goodreads.

READ MORE from PEGGY

Peggy is the author of the popular Southern Cousins Mysteries, a comedic cozy series starring Elvis, the hound dog who thinks he's the King of Rock 'n' Roll reincarnated. Get her latest!

ELVIS AND THE BLUE SUEDE BONES

The Valentine family has received BIG NEWS and everybody's in a fever. While Ruby Nell (Mama) throws a garden party to spread the news, Elvis is in her flower beds digging up some blue suede bones – human bones. Suspicious minds put the blame on Mama. Callie and cousin Lovie go into sleuth mode along with everybody's favorite crooning canine detective. Can Elvis and the Valentine gang catch a killer with murder always on his mind before Ruby Nell ends up singing the jailhouse rock?

Peggy also writes women's fiction beloved by her fans for her portrayal of female friendships and family. Get her two latest novels now. For a complete list of her books, visit her website - www.peggywebb.com.

STARS TO LEAD ME HOME

Sometimes you have to lose everything to find your true home.

If you've ever tried to pick up the pieces after a marriage goes up in smoke, you'll know Maggie. If you've ever thought your daughter might not speak to you again or a life-threatening illness would claim your best friend, you'll understand Maggie's heart. And if you've ever wished on a star, you'll cheer for her throughout this book.

"It's the kind of book you can't wait to share with

friends."

A NECESSARY WOMAN

"Fans of THE HELP and SAVING CEE CEE HONEYCUT will love this book!"

Tamara Tillman

A mother looking for a miracle. An outcast looking for a home. And the remarkable dog who brings them together.

In the last summer of Camelot, President Kennedy urged a nation toward unity. In November he was struck down by an assassin's bullet. Against that backdrop of enormous hope and great heartbreak, a teenaged girl whose only family is a stray dog named Catfish and a desperate mother whose only living child seems broken beyond repair discover the true meaning of family and of grace.

Thank you for reading the BREAKDOWN series! Your reviews will help other readers discover these page-turning novels. I hope you will consider leaving reviews of all four BREAKDOWN books on Amazon.